# "A marriage of convenience... a business deal!"

"You get a partner to stand next to you on platforms and say the right things at civic functions," Paige continued, "I get the vineyard back in a year?"

Brad nodded. "We'd be sleeping partners for a year." The gleam of humor in his eyes made her hands curl into tight fists at her sides.

"You mean a marriage in name only?"

He didn't answer her immediately. His eyes moved over her, looking at the curves of her figure, the luxuriant fall of her hair around the young face. "No, I know my limitations. You do have a fabulous body and I have a very healthy appetite. I'd want you in my bed, Paige."

Dear Reader,

Welcome to

Everyone has special occasions in their life—times of celebration and excitement. Maybe it's a romantic event—an engagement or a wedding—or perhaps a wonderful family occasion, such as the birth of a baby. Or even a personal milestone—a thirtieth or fortieth birthday!

These are all important times in our lives and in THE BIG EVENT! you can see how different couples react to these events. Whatever the occasion, romance and drama are guaranteed!

We've been featuring some terrific stories from some of your favorite authors. If you've enjoyed this miniseries in Harlequin Romance®, we hope you'll continue to look out for THE BIG EVENT! in Harlequin Presents®. This month, we're delighted to bring you **Bride for a Year** by Kathryn Ross. In October, we have bestselling author Penny Jordan's **Marriage Make Up**—will a divorced couple be reunited at their daughter's wedding?

Happy reading!

The Editors

# KATHRYN ROSS

## Bride for a Year

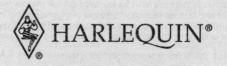

TORONTO • NEW YORK • LONDON
AMSTERDAM • PARIS • SYDNEY • HAMBURG
STOCKHOLM • ATHENS • TOKYO • MILAN • MADRID
PRAGUE • WARSAW • BUDAPEST • AUCKLAND

ISBN 0-373-11981-X

BRIDE FOR A YEAR

First North American Publication 1998.

# CHAPTER ONE

THE last rays of sunshine were slanting across the Californian vineyard as Paige stopped work for the day. She stood up and dusted down her jeans as she surveyed her handiwork.

She was a slender woman of twenty-two, with long, dark hair, her delicate, feminine appearance totally at odds with her work clothes and the heavy toolbox she had been using. She wasn't much good at DIY, but despite this she had made a reasonable job of fixing the fence. The only problem was that it had taken her so long.

It was the same with every task she had undertaken that day. She had started work at six in the morning and hadn't stopped, yet she still had several jobs that had been on her list of things to do today. She sighed. The light was fading fast so she would just have to leave everything until the morning. Besides, she was too tired to continue. All she could dream about now was a long, luxurious bath in scented hot water.

The thought made her start to pack her work gear away with haste. She was just finishing when she heard the sound of a horse's hooves on the hard, dusty driveway. She turned and her heart hammered crazily as she saw her neighbour, Brad Monroe, riding up towards her.

She had been expecting him for a while now; she knew what he had come to say. Apprehension knotted inside her.

'Good evening, Paige.' He reined in the powerful black stallion just beside her.

'Evening.' It took a supreme effort to sound indifferent to him.

'How are things going?'

The casual question made her temper simmer. As if he cared! She turned and threw the last of her work things back in the box. 'Not bad...considering,' she muttered as she fastened the lid on the box.

He waited until she had finished. His horse pawed at the ground as if impatient with the delay, but Brad's voice was very relaxed as he commented, 'If you'd asked, I'd have sent someone over to help you with that fence.'

She flicked him a disparaging look from glimmering blue eyes. 'I don't need any help from you.'

'Hell, Paige, you are one stubborn woman.' A note of impatience crept into his voice now.

She ignored that and bent to pick up the box of tools, her long, dark hair falling silkily over her face. The box was heavy but she put a determined effort into not showing it. Her slender body protested against the weight and she was forced to use both hands.

She heard the creak of the saddle leather as he dismounted.

She looked at him as he walked towards her. The final, dying rays of red sun slanted across him like a spotlight. He was tall, well over six feet, with thick, dark hair, a square jawline and eyes that were so dark they reminded her of burnt toffee. He was thirty seven, fifteen years older than she, and he looked like a movie star even in his faded jeans and denim shirt.

Paige felt her heart thud uncomfortably. She had always found Brad extremely attractive. From first laying eyes on him when she was thirteen she had imagined herself in love with him, had secretly dreamed that one day he would look at her and feel the same way. That had never happened. Just as well, she told herself fiercely now, because Brad Monroe was not the man she had built him up to be. Just a few months ago she had found out what kind of a person he really was and all her illusions had been swept away.

He reached to take the heavy box from her and his hand closed over hers. The touch of his skin against hers made tiny darts of awareness shoot through her, and heat flooded through her body.

Their eyes met for just a moment before she pulled away, allowing him to take the box from her.

'I suppose you have come to give me an ultimatum: pay up the money I owe you or get out.' Her voice wasn't entirely steady and that annoyed her. She didn't want him to know that she wasn't perfectly in control around him.

'I'm not your enemy, Paige,' he said coolly. 'I've only ever wanted to help you.'

'You've only ever wanted to get your hands on this land,' she corrected him cuttingly. 'Forgive me for being blunt, Brad, but your caring neighbour act no longer impresses me. I know what your real motives are. You're a vulture, and finally, after all these months of circling, you are about to swoop in for the pickings. I've been expecting you for weeks now.'

He shook his head. 'I know you are still in shock after your father's death. You are not seeing things clearly yet, but—'

'The problem is I can see things too clearly,' she interrupted him. 'Now, if you will excuse me, I've had a long, tiring day and I want to go inside my house and relax.' While she still had a house to relax in... The words remained unspoken at the back of her mind.

Instead of leaving as she had hoped, he fell into step beside her as she walked up towards the house.

'If it helps to blame me then go ahead,' he said in a low tone. 'But sooner rather than later you are going to have to face the truth. It's two months since your father died. You can't carry on here on your own for much longer. The vineyard is falling down around you, Paige. It is going to take a lot of money to put things right and you haven't got it. Not only that, but you are vastly in debt.'

Paige didn't want to hear his assessment of her problems. Her pride rebelled furiously against it, but she said nothing because deep down she knew that he was right.

'Look, Paige, I haven't come over here to upset you. I've come to offer some practical help. If you want, I'll sit down with you, help you go through your accounts—'

She laughed at that. 'So you can get some inside knowledge on how much you can steal my vineyard from me for? No, thanks. My accounts are my own business.'

Silence fell between them. Velvet darkness had enveloped the countryside. The air was hot and heavy with the tropical sound of cicadas. The smell of the parched earth was broken by the sweetness of the eucalyptus trees which shaded the white, colonial-style house that had been Paige's home since she was thirteen.

She took a long, deep breath. She loved this place, with all its familiar sights and scents. She loved everything about it. But she knew that she had lost it...knew that her dream of holding onto it, of working on her own to save it, had been illogical in the extreme.

Brad put her box down on the porch that encircled the house. 'Whatever you might think, I am concerned about you.'

'You're concerned because you've had to wait longer than you had envisioned to get your hands on this estate. All you can think about is extending your vineyard and your profits.'

He caught hold of her arm as she made to swing away

from him. 'I did not cause your father's financial problems.'

'Maybe not,' she muttered tightly. 'But you sure as hell speeded up his downfall.'

'By lending him money when he most needed it?' Brad's voice was droll.

'By demanding it back in an impossibly short time. You may not have started my father's problems, but you certainly finished him.' Paige's eyes blazed into his. 'You come here telling me that you are not the enemy, but in my eyes you are...and you always will be. You could have afforded to give my father longer to pay you back but you didn't. You contributed to his death and I hate you for it.'

'That's vastly unreasonable, Paige.' His voice was low with fury, but none-the-less very cutting. 'Yes, all right, I could have afforded to let the loan ride longer, but I didn't see the point. Your father was a fool who...' He hesitated and she finished the words for him.

'Who wasn't as ruthless in business as he should have been?' Her eyes shone with vivid, intense light at that. 'At least he was honourable.'

'And you think I'm not?'

'I know what you are. I've seen the real you in action these last few months.' She looked down at the hand he had on her arm her manner very cold. 'Now let go of me.'

'Paige, we need to talk and sort this out,' he said harshly.

'There's nothing to discuss.'

'Like hell there is.' He pulled her closer to his body and the contact made her temperature rise dramatically. 'We've been friends and neighbours for years. I won't have you turning our familys' friendship into some kind of dramatic vendetta...which is all in your mind. You were away at college when your father's...financial problems got out of hand and he came to me for an extension of the time limit on his loan. You don't know the real facts.'

'I know what my father told me,' she blazed furiously. 'I know when I came home and went across to your house and asked you again, for my father, would you extend the time limit you more or less laughed in my face. Or are you going to try and tell me I imagined that as well?'

'I gave you my reasons for not extending the time limit on the loan,' he said calmly.

'Yes, you did... Now, what did you say?' She rolled her eyes disdainfully. 'Oh, yes, it was for his own good.' Her voice grated sarcastically. 'Very helpful of you, I must say.'

'Matt was in way over his head, Paige. You don't fully understand the problem.'

'Don't patronise me, Brad.' Her tone was brittle.

'That wasn't my intention. What I meant was that you were away at college, you didn't see what was happening here—'

'Now you are trying to tell me it was all my fault, because I haven't been living at home for a few years.' She shook her head. 'You must be really desperate for this place. What's the matter, Brad? Is your sojourn into the world of politics costing you more money than you'd thought? Are you seeking to extend your profit margins by stealing my land?'

'The fact that I'm running for mayor has nothing to do with this. Except for the fact that I'd rather not have the hassle of you going around bad mouthing me.'

'Frightened people might not vote for you if they knew how you'd treated my father?' Her voice grated. 'I'm not surprised you're worried. The truth isn't exactly good for the image you like to project, is it? That caring "I'm only doing this for the community" spiel rings very hollow next to the way you've treated your neighbour.'

He shook his head. 'I can't believe how you are twisting the facts.'

'It's the truth, Brad, and you know it.'

'The truth as you see it. Blinkered and inaccurate.'

She shook her head. 'I know the only reason you lent my father that money in the first place was the hope that he wouldn't be able to pay you back, that it enabled you to get your hooks into this property. I'm sure when I put the place on the market you will be the one picking it up for next to nothing.'

'Are you considering selling?'

'Careful, Brad, your thirst for blood is showing.' Her lips twisted, the fire inside her starting to die. 'And, yes, of course I'm going to sell. I do know when I'm beaten. I shall put the estate on the open market next week. I've been advised that an auction is my best bet; then I can disappear into the wide blue yonder and start a new life.'

He frowned.

'Oh, don't worry. I'll settle my debts with you out of the proceeds of the sale before I leave California,' she assured him.

'Where will you go?' She felt his surprise, almost palpable in the air between them.

'Depends how much money you deign to leave me with. I know that whoever buys it will get it at a knockdown price. It's not in the best of conditions any longer.'

'My fault again, I presume?' he muttered dryly.

'Your words, not mine.' Her glance slanted away from him to where his horse was standing, idly munching at the greenery over the white picket fence that separated the garden from the vineyard. 'And your horse certainly isn't helping matters.'

'It's a conspiracy, no doubt,' Brad said as he moved to catch hold of the animal's bridle. 'I'm out to ruin your life and I've told Buck to work his way through your garden.' There was a gleam of humour in Brad's dark eyes as he looked at her.

For just a second she wanted to smile with him. The memory of how relaxed she used to feel around him, of how he had always been able to make her laugh, was there very strongly in her heart.

'We used to be friends, Paige,' he said quietly as she continued just to stare at him.

Her heart thumped very unevenly. 'Did we?' She shook her head. 'I can't remember that.'

Then she turned away from him and hurried up the steps towards the front door, allowing the fly screen and the door to bang noisily behind her as she closed it.

She didn't turn on the lights in the hallway immediately. Instead, she stood in the darkness, her back against the door, her breathing uneven.

'We used to be friends...' Brad's words drummed through her and with them memories flicked like photographs through her mind.

From being a young girl she had looked up to Brad, respected him...loved him. At least he had never guessed at her true feelings for him; that would be too humiliating. To Brad she was just the girl next door; that was where his thoughts of friendship started and finished.

She remembered how, as a teenager, he had teased her mercilessly and yet always made her laugh...always melted her with one look from those incredible eyes of his.

She had yearned to be old enough to go out with him, had felt quite jealous of the succession of glamorous women in his life.

His mother had guessed the truth, though. Thinking about Elizabeth brought a lump to her throat.

Paige couldn't remember her own mother, but

Elizabeth was everything she would have wished her to be. Kind, amusing, open. Paige had felt able to talk to her…had enjoyed her company.

It had been Brad's mother who had taught her to ride; she had talked to her about the land, about the grape-vines; it had been she rather than her own father who had instilled a love of the land into her.

It was eighteen months since Elizabeth had died and Paige still missed her. Her hands curled into tight fists at her sides. Lord alone knew what she would make of this situation now.

Briskly she started to walk across the dark hallway. She didn't want to think about the past; she was too tired, too tearful. She would go upstairs, have her bath and forget everything. Her thoughts broke off as she hit her foot quite violently against a solid, sharp object. She cried out instinctively as pain shot through her, then sank down on the floor to rub her injury, tears of anger and frustration in her eyes.

'Damn, damn, damn,' she muttered under her breath. She had forgotten that earlier today she had dragged some tea chests down from the attic and left them in the centre of the hall.

'Paige, are you OK?'

Brad's voice from outside the front door was very unwelcome.

'Yes. Go away,' she called out, wanting to be left alone.

He ignored her completely and she heard the door open. The next moment the overhead light flicked on.

He came quickly across to her, an expression of concern on the handsome features. 'What the heck have you done?'

'I was playing football and a tea chest fell on me,' she muttered sarcastically.

'You always were a bit of a tomboy,' he grinned as

he bent down and pushed up her jeans to have a look at her foot.

She winced with pain as his fingers touched her flesh. 'You'll live… You've just bruised yourself.' He straightened and for a moment she thought he was just going to leave. Instead, he walked away in the direction of the kitchen. 'I'll get you some ice to put on it.'

'There's no need. I'll manage on my own.' She stood up and found her foot still throbbed too much to put her full weight on it, so she leaned against the chest.

He came back with a tea towel filled with ice cubes and knelt down beside her to put it against her foot.

For some reason his gentleness filled her with a feeling of acute sadness. She looked down at the darkness of his hair and for a moment was overcome by an irrational desire to touch him, to reach out a hand and stroke it through the soft thickness of that hair.

'Feel any better?' He looked up at her and she nodded.

'Thank you.' Her voice was husky.

He straightened and looked at her.

Paige could feel her anger against him evaporating in a wave of stronger emotion, a feeling that this was the man she had always loved…always looked up to. Sorrow filled her blue eyes, darkening them to the shade of deepest violet. If only her father hadn't turned to Brad for financial help, she thought miserably. She didn't want to think badly of Brad; she wanted to push all those thoughts away and turn to him as she had always felt able to turn to him in the past, trust him as she had always trusted him.

His eyes lingered gently on her face. 'I hate to see you so sad, Paige; it tears me apart.'

She swallowed hard. She wouldn't cry, she told herself staunchly. 'You…you should have thought of that when my father asked you to extend your time limit.' Her words held none of the accusing tones of before;

now her voice was just filled with regret. 'All we needed was a couple more months—'

He shook his head. His eyes moved around the hallway, taking in the large tea chests cluttering the area. 'I never wanted it to come to this,' he muttered grimly. 'I certainly had no idea that you were already starting to pack things up. I had thought it would be a while yet before you came to that.' He raked a distracted hand through his hair. 'It will be a mammoth task packing everything from this house.'

She nodded. 'Three generations of my family have lived here. It will take me some time to sort everything out.'

'What will you do? Put it in storage?'

She shrugged. 'The real-estate people have advised me to sell everything. But there are a number of things that are of great sentimental value so I'll sort through and take what I can.' She tried to sound practical, tried not to let him know that this was breaking her heart.

'You love this place so much, don't you?' he asked softly.

She took a deep breath. 'It's my home...'

His eyes met hers. 'No matter what you might think, this isn't what I wanted,' he said softly. 'Just for the record, it was my mother who first lent your father the money he needed, not me,' he said calmly. 'And she did it out of a desire to help. She was very fond of you, Paige.'

The words stilled her. 'I was fond of her, too.' For a moment tears shimmered in the bright blue of her eyes. 'And it was very kind of her,' she admitted huskily.

'Don't cry, Paige.'

'I'm not crying,' she denied angrily, brushing away a tear as it dared to trickle over the smooth pallor of her skin.

He moved closer and folded her into the warmth of

his arms. For a moment she leaned against him, breathing in the comfort of being held. Then she looked up at him and subtly the feelings of grief changed to an awareness of him and the way he was holding her.

He breathed her name in a whisper-soft way that made her skin prickle with consciousness. She wanted him to kiss her; the desire that flared inside her was so strong it was overwhelming.

Then his head lowered and she felt his lips against the cool salt of her tears, caressing warmth back to her body, stirring feelings of desire and need alive with vivid intensity.

For years she had secretly dreamed that one day he would kiss her. She had imagined that it would be passionate, but she hadn't been prepared for the storm of desire it unleashed.

When he moved back from her she was breathless. She stared wordlessly up into the darkness of his eyes.

Then reality crashed around her. She thought about her father, thought about the broken words he had murmured to her, the words of hate against Brad Monroe. 'Cold, hard, ruthless', he had called him. The words drummed through her mind like a reproach and she felt heavy with guilt, her passion for Brad somehow seeming a vast disloyalty to her father's memory.

She pushed him away from her. 'I don't know why that happened, but it was a big mistake.'

One dark eyebrow lifted. 'I thought it was quite enjoyable myself,' he murmured flippantly.

'I don't suppose your girlfriend would be quite so amused,' Paige said tersely.

'I don't have a girlfriend,' Brad retorted. 'So it's nobody's business but my own.'

Paige frowned. She knew for a fact that Brad was dating Carolyn Murphy. He had been seeing her for the last six months and most people were expecting the sound of wedding bells. 'So what about Carolyn?' she enquired.

'Carolyn and I have split up.'

'But I thought... Everyone thought that you two were, well, going to get married.'

His eyebrows rose even further at that. 'Everyone takes a lot for granted around here,' he muttered dryly. 'But no, it's all over between Carolyn and me.'

'Oh!' She stared at him, really startled by this news. 'Are you upset?'

Brad's lips twisted. 'Why, do you want to comfort me?' he drawled sardonically. 'A few more kisses like that one and I might start to feel a heck of a lot better.'

'Don't be absurd.' Her heart missed several beats. It didn't matter whom he was involved with, how free he might be, she told herself fiercely. She wasn't interested. And yet a small part of her was remembering that kiss...remembering how good it had felt to be in his arms.

She turned away from him. 'I think you should go now.'

'If that's what you want.' Silence fell between them. 'I hope you'll believe me, Paige, when I tell you that I never intended to ruin your father.'

She didn't say anything to that...didn't know what to think any more. She was bewildered and scared and had never felt more alone in her life.

'If it will help, I want you to know that I can wait for the money you owe me. It doesn't matter when you pay it back.'

She spun around at that. 'I can't believe you!' she said with a stunned shake of her head. 'Just a few months ago I begged you to extend our time limit. You refused point-blank. Now my father is dead and you have the audacity to calmly tell me it doesn't matter when I pay you back.'

'I want to help you.'

'Well, it's too late.' Her voice was anguished now. 'And you know damned well it is.'

'I can't stand by and watch you go to the wall,' he muttered.

'At the risk of repeating myself, you were willing to stand by and do just that a few months ago.' She took a deep breath. 'Either you've got a massively guilty conscience or you're a damn good actor.'

'I don't have a guilty conscience,' he told her swiftly. 'I had my reasons for refusing your father. They were good reasons.'

'So good that I can't understand them,' she snapped. 'Well, I'm not so unintelligent that I don't see behind this charade of an offer now.' She put one hand on her hip. 'You are bothered about what people will think if I blab about the details of my father's financial problems. A man who is running for mayor wouldn't want this kind of blot on his copybook. So you come over here with the grand, charitable gesture of letting me off the hook a while longer.' She shook her head. 'I don't need or want your charity, Brad.'

'I'm not offering you charity,' he rasped dryly. 'I'm extending the hand of a concerned neighbour—'

'Oh, please!' She cut across him with laughing disdain. 'As you are well aware, Brad, it's too little, too late. That's the problem when you're heading towards bankruptcy, you see...' Her voice shook with derision. 'It's like a domino effect. You get behind with one debt then others pile up... Then someone demands their money immediately and one by one things start to collapse.' She glared at him. 'I'm the last domino standing in place and all I can do is sell up fast before I fall flat on my face. You offering, oh, so benevolently, to prop me up for a little while longer won't make a scrap of difference now. I needed your support several months ago... It's no damn good to me at all now.'

'Things are that bad, then?' he asked quietly.

She slanted him a dry look. 'You were the one telling me how bad things were as we walked in from the vineyard.'

'I didn't realise that things had moved quite so quickly.' He shook his head. 'Have you spoken with the bank?'

She nodded and bent to lift the icepack from her foot. It had stopped throbbing now, maybe overshadowed by the greater pain inside. 'They strongly urge me to go ahead with the auction...and not to waste a moment.'

'Can't you just sell off pieces of the property, without losing your house?' he asked. 'I'd be interested in acquiring some of your land.'

'I'm sure you would.' She flashed him a knowing look. 'I knew that's what you were angling for—'

'That's not what I want,' he cut in tersely.

'So which piece of land are you thinking of?' she carried on swiftly, as if he hadn't spoken.

He shrugged. 'How about the slice that runs along the far back of my property?'

'You mean the piece that contains the only water I have?' Her voice trembled with fury. 'This place won't fetch very much on the open market, not in this run-down state, but without that water it will be virtually worthless.'

'You can modernise. Install a new irrigation system in—'

'Do you have any idea how much money you are talking about?' she demanded fiercely.

'Of course,' he replied coolly.

'Then you'll know that even if I did sell you that land there wouldn't be enough left over from paying back my debt to you and the others to install a bore hole, never mind anything else.' She raked a hand through her hair. 'No, I'll have to sell the whole place... There's no alternative.'

She swung away from him and walked over towards the kitchen to put the rapidly melting ice in the sink. For a moment her eyes moved over the rustic charm of the place. The dresser, the pine scrubbed table and the dried flowers on the farmhouse rack... Her home. Her heart twisted painfully.

'So where will you go?'

Brad's voice in the doorway behind her made her turn and look at him.

She shrugged. 'I've got friends that I made when I was away at college. I've had letters of condolence and an offer that I can share a friend's flat while I look around for a job.'

'A male friend?' Brad asked, a caustic note in his voice.

She frowned. The offer had been from a girlfriend, but she wasn't about to enlighten him. 'That's none of your damned business,' she grated with annoyance. 'The fact remains that I have very little option but to move away from this area altogether. I need to get myself a job, start again.'

'There are always other options.'

'Such as?'

'We could become partners,' he said quietly.

She was so surprised she could hardly say anything for a moment. 'You mean you would write off my loan and straighten out all my other debts if I made you a sleeping partner in the vineyard?'

'In a roundabout way...yes.'

She was incredulous now. 'You do want the vineyard, then?'

He shrugged. 'I'm more in need of the partner than I am of the vineyard.'

When she continued to stare at him, perplexed, he smiled. 'I need a wife.'

'A wife?' She looked at him blankly. 'I'm sorry, Brad, I don't understand.'

'I'm asking you to marry me,' he said quietly.

She stared at him. This had to be some kind of a joke! Her lips curved and she found herself laughing. She couldn't help herself. It was the nerve-tingling absurdity of the suggestion. 'You can't possibly be serious!'

'I'm not talking about a lifelong commitment. I'm talking about twelve months.'

'It sounds like a jail sentence.' Paige was rewarded by a momentary expression of anger on his face. It gave her a certain amount of pleasure to strike through that cool, smug exterior of his. What on earth was he playing at? she wondered grimly. She had no illusions about his feelings for her... They might have been friends in the past, but he had never given her any indication that he wanted that friendship to deepen, no matter how much she had secretly yearned for it.

'You want me for twelve months... What do I get?' she asked derisively. 'A purple heart for living with the enemy?'

'You get this place. I'll build it up for you, stick it back together and write off your loans.' His voice was tight.

'That's a pretty expensive package.' Her heart thundered against her breast. 'And you'd be willing to do that to have me as your wife for twelve months?' She shook her head. 'I don't understand this at all. Why a year? What's in it for you?'

His lips curved in a mirthless smile. 'I want a dutiful wife... Someone who will look up at me adoringly.'

Suddenly it clicked with her. 'This is all because you are running for mayor here, isn't it? You want the right image? The loving husband, a family man—'

'Hold on there.' He cut across her swiftly. 'I'm not looking to start a family with you… Children are not part of the equation.'

Heat licked through her at the insulting undertone of that statement, but before she could coherently formulate a cutting reply he continued, 'But yes, it has been suggested that I will find it easier to get elected if I'm married.'

'And when we part… How would that look to your precious image?'

He laughed. 'I'll tell everyone you married me for my money… It won't be so far from the truth, will it? I'll probably be voted in again out of sympathy.'

She shook her head. 'So why me?'

'Why not you? You're attractive. You know the score up front. We can draw up a business agreement and know where we stand.' He shrugged. 'I'm not really the marrying kind. I like my freedom. However, twelve months doesn't sound like such a bad idea.'

It was such a preposterous idea that she just stared at him. 'A marriage of convenience…a business deal,' she muttered finally. 'You get a partner to stand next to you on platforms and say the right things at civic functions, I get the vineyard back in a year?'

He nodded. 'We'd be sleeping partners for a year.' The gleam of humour in his eyes made her hands curl into tight fists at her sides.

'You mean a marriage in name only?'

He didn't answer her immediately. His eyes moved over her, looking at the curves of her figure, the luxuriant fall of her hair around the young face.

'No, I know my limitations. You do have a fabulous body and I have a very healthy appetite. I'd want you in my bed, Paige.'

For just a moment she was so shocked that she couldn't speak.

'It's not such a repulsive idea...is it, Paige?' he enquired genuinely. 'I know you are a good deal younger than I, but when we kissed a few moments ago it was very pleasurable; you can't deny that. In fact I'm sure I tasted desire on your lips. It made me wonder why I had never kissed you before.'

Her skin burned with furious fires of humiliation and anger. The fact that he was right just served to infuriate her further. Her pride would never admit to the fact that she found him attractive...never. She shook her head. 'That's in your imagination. You tasted surprise, shock, nothing else.'

One dark eyebrow lifted. 'Are you sure? There was a time when I wondered if you might have a crush on me.'

The arrogance of that remark really stung. 'How far back are you going?' She kept her equilibrium with difficulty. 'You're not going to remind me of the time I invited you to be my date for my high-school prom, are you?' She forced herself to laugh. She knew very well that this was one of the few times she had braved showing her feelings to Brad, had allowed herself to flirt. 'Heavens! If I remember rightly you laughed, told me that people would accuse you of robbing the cradle, and you were right, it was absurd.' She added flippantly, 'I must just have been into older men at the time.'

He shrugged. 'You were very young.'

'The same fifteen years are still between us,' she said, quietly now.

'I haven't forgotten.' His voice was heavy, very serious for a moment. Then his eyes moved over the slender lines of her figure. 'But you are twenty-two now and it's different.'

For just a second Paige gained the impression that he was trying to convince himself of this fact more than her.

'I'm fair game to be exploited for a year, you mean?'

she snapped, her nerves stretching beyond endurance. 'I'd rather sell my soul to the devil.' Her voice trembled.

'I wouldn't call being pulled from the brink of bankruptcy exploitation.' He laughed at that. 'And I think you will agree to my proposal...because it will be the most profitable move of your life.' He turned and walked towards the door. 'Think it over.'

# CHAPTER TWO

'I CAN'T believe that you are faced with the prospect of selling this place,' Rosie said with heartfelt sympathy in her voice.

'It's just unfortunate.' Paige tried to play down her emotion on the subject as she poured her friend another cup of coffee.

They were in Paige's kitchen at the vineyard. It was getting up towards midday and Paige had a million jobs waiting to be done. She had shelved them all very gratefully when Rosie arrived, glad of a chance to talk and relax for a while.

'But what will you do? Where will you go?'

Paige shrugged. At the back of her mind Brad's offer lay...too scary to think deeply about, too intriguing to forget. 'I might go to Seattle. One of my friends has got a flat up there and apparently some contacts if I want to start looking for a job.'

'Seattle!' Rosie sounded shocked. 'That's a hell of a long way away... Who lives up there? Not that guy you were friendly with...Josh Summers?'

Paige smiled. 'No, not Josh. He was just a friend, you know, Rosie... There was nothing romantic between us.'

'No, but he would have liked there to be. I saw the way he looked at you when he came up here for that long weekend.'

'He was just a fellow student. I had a card of sympathy from him when he heard about my father's death...but I certainly have no plans to move in with him, I can assure you.' She leaned back against the windowsill and sighed. 'Strange, but Brad jumped to exactly the same conclusion when I told him I might share a flat with a friend. He asked if it was a male friend.'

'Did he, now?' Rosie looked extremely interested in this. 'When did you see Brad?'

'He came over here last night.' For a moment there was silence as Paige grappled with her conscience over whether or not to tell Rosie about Brad's outrageous proposal.

Paige had been friends with Rosie Jefferson for years. They used to sit together in school, and had shared many secrets and dreams over the years. Even though they had been separated while Paige was away at college, and Rosie got married, they were still as close as ever.

But now, for the first time, Paige found she didn't want to confide in her friend. It wasn't that she didn't trust Rosie, it was more that she didn't want to voice the extremely personal nature of Brad's proposal—the fact that he had suggested a relationship based purely on business reasons hurt in some strange way. She tried to tell herself that it was her pride that was hurting, but deep down she wasn't too sure.

'Have you forgiven him over the money?' Rosie asked, her eyes moving over the pallor of Paige's skin.

She shrugged. 'I suppose if, I'm honest, I can't really blame him totally... What is it they say? Never a lender or a borrower be?'

'I'm sure if he could have afforded to let your father's loan ride he would have,' Rosie said with a nod. 'He's a decent guy.'

'Yes...' Deep down Paige wanted to believe that. But the fact that Brad had openly told her he could afford to let the loan ride and had chosen not to did still grate rawly. Her father had been so broken up just before he had died... The memory was pitiful and it tore at Paige.

'I'm glad that you two are friends again,' Rosie continued briskly. 'Brad must be pretty upset at the moment, anyway. I believe he and Carolyn Murphy have split up.'

'He mentioned something,' Paige said noncommittally.

'Apparently she has ditched him for Robert Hicks.'

'Really?' There was complete amazement in Paige's voice now. Strangely she hadn't for one moment considered the fact that Carolyn might have been the one to finish with Brad.

Rosie grinned. 'I knew that would surprise you. You've always had a soft spot for Brad, haven't you?'

'That's in the past.' Paige tried to sound firmly convinced and ignore the little whispering voice inside her that wanted to argue with that.

'Sure.' Rosie wasn't at all taken in by Paige's reply. 'But you're right, Carolyn must have been crazy to finish with Brad; he is gorgeous. If I weren't a married woman, and didn't adore my Mike, I'd be interested myself.'

'How do you know that Carolyn finished with him? Did Brad tell you that?'

'No, of course not. Mike sees a lot of Brad these days as he's going to be managing Brad's campaign for mayor. But I don't think they discuss things like that... Well, if they do, my husband certainly hasn't repeated it to me. No, I met Carolyn in town a while ago and she told me herself.' Rose wrinkled her nose. 'She's extremely confident, you know, and I must say she looked fabulous. Made me wish I'd stuck to my diet last year.'

'You don't need to diet, Rosie,' Paige said quickly. Rosie Jefferson was an extremely attractive blonde. She wasn't fat, she just had a curvaceous figure.

Rosie shrugged as if she didn't agree but wasn't going to argue about it today.

'So what did Carolyn say?' Paige reached to pick up her coffee from the table.

'Get this.' Rosie's eyes twinkled with good humour.

'She said, and I quote, ''I've finished with Brad. He was getting rather tiresome. Robert has asked me to marry him and I've accepted.'''

'Marry him!' Paige's eyes widened. 'She's marrying Robert Hicks!'

'Just goes to show you can't take anything for granted.' Rosie nodded. 'I think we were all convinced that Carolyn would marry Brad. They seemed like the perfect couple, didn't they?'

'Yes, they did,' Paige agreed quietly.

'Of course, Robert comes from an extremely wealthy family. They own a lot of property in San Francisco. Carolyn was telling me that they are going to live there after the wedding.'

Paige wondered if deep down Brad was heartsore about the whole thing.

'Anyway, the coast is now clear. As far as I can make out Brad isn't seeing anyone at the moment…not a girl-friend on the playing field.'

'I'm sure that won't be the situation for very long.' Paige sipped her coffee then met the gleam in her friend's eye. 'Don't look at me like that. I'm not in the slightest bit interested any more,' she said staunchly.

Yet despite the strong words, despite everything that had happened to turn her against Brad, she knew very well that she was far more interested than she should be. She wondered if the fact that Carolyn had finished with Brad had triggered his decision to propose to her. Perhaps he had been counting on Carolyn to be by his side during the elections and now that the love of his life was going to marry someone else he had decided just to cut his losses and make a marriage purely for business reasons. 'Anyway, once this place is sold I shall be moving away. So it's irrelevant who Brad is seeing or isn't seeing,' she said firmly, trying very hard not to care.

Rosie frowned. 'You aren't really serious about leaving the valley, Paige? Surely you could find a job around here? You've only just graduated from college; you've got bags of qualifications.'

Paige shook her head. 'I'm going to make a fresh start,' she said with gentle determination. 'I couldn't bear to stay around here and see this vineyard being run by someone else. It would just break my heart.'

'I don't want you to leave, Paige...' Rosie looked over at her, a sudden serious light in her eyes. 'Especially now.'

'Believe me, I don't want to go—' Paige broke off and frowned at her friend. 'Why especially now?'

'I was going to ask you to be godmother to our baby.' Rosie smiled, happiness radiating through her every word.

'Rosie! You're not!' Paige put her cup down and squealed with delight.

'I am.' Rosie nodded. 'Four weeks pregnant.'

Paige moved to throw her arms around her friend.

'It just seems that everything is going right at last,' Rosie said, her eyes misting with sudden tears.

'Oh, Rosie, it's wonderful news. I'm so happy for you both.' Paige squeezed her friend warmly before drawing back.

'So you can't go away...not now,' Rosie said earnestly. 'I want you to stay. I want you to settle down here and be as happy as Mike and I are.'

'I don't think that's possible,' Paige said with a tremor in her voice.

'Anything is possible,' Rosie said with strong conviction.

The sound of a car driving up outside made Rosie break off. Paige went to glance out of the window. A bright red Porsche had pulled in alongside Rosie's old car and her Jeep.

'It's Brad,' Paige murmured, her body filling with sudden apprehension.

'Anybody home?' His voice, strong and decisive, filtered through from the front hallway a moment later.

'He acts as if he owns the place already,' Paige said with annoyance. 'Just barges on in when it suits him.'

Rosie smiled. 'We are in the kitchen, Brad,' she called out cheerfully.

A few seconds later he appeared in the kitchen doorway, looking tanned and powerfully attractive in his jeans and a navy blue polo shirt. 'It seems I've arrived just in time,' he grinned, eyeing the coffee pot on the table.

'You certainly have.' Rosie was the one who got out another cup and poured the drink for him. 'Good to see you, Brad.'

'It's good to see you too...and looking so well.' He smiled and kissed the side of Rosie's cheek as he passed her. 'I've just come from your house. Mike was telling me the good news. Congratulations.'

Rosie's cheeks flared a bright pink. 'Thanks.'

Brad glanced over at Paige and for a moment his dark eyes lingered contemplatively on her face.

She felt heat licking through her veins as she remembered their last meeting, the way he'd kissed her...his proposal.

She looked hurriedly away from him, but she was still acutely aware of the way he was watching her, the way his eyes had travelled away from her face and down over the slender lines of her figure in the pale blue sundress.

Rosie handed him his coffee. 'Actually, I was just leaving,' she said, looking from him towards Paige.

'You don't have to dash off on my account,' Brad said sipping his drink.

'No, no, I was going anyway.' Rosie finished her coffee. 'Perhaps you can talk some sense into Paige. She's talking about going to live in Seattle, you know.'

'Seattle?' Brad looked at Paige with a frown.

Silence hung heavily in the air for a moment before Rosie said with a gleam of mischief in her eyes. 'She won't admit it, but I'm sure it's that guy she met at college trying to talk her into going up there. Probably hoping she'll agree to live with him.'

'Rosie!' Paige's eyes widened at such a blatant untruth.

'It isn't good to make such a radical decision while you are still in mourning for your father, Paige... You're not thinking clearly,' Rosie continued totally unabashed by the look of disapproval on her friend's face. She reached to pick up her handbag. 'Anyway, I'll leave you two alone. As I said, perhaps you can talk some sense into her Brad...?'

'Thank you, but I don't need anyone to talk sense into me,' Paige murmured uncomfortably. 'I am quite capable of managing my own life.'

Rosie shook her head. 'I'll phone you later, Paige. Let's have lunch one day next week?'

Paige nodded and made to walk to the car with her friend, but Rosie waved her hand. 'I can find my own way.'

The silence in the kitchen was loaded with tension once the back door closed behind her.

'Seattle?' Brad said again, and shook his head. 'You know it does nothing but rain up there, don't you?'

'It will make a refreshing change, then, won't it?' Paige said briskly. She finished her coffee and put the cup down on the pine kitchen table, her eyes moving to the perfect blue sky outside.

'Is there some man waiting in the wings for you up there?' Brad persisted.

'I've told you once, that's none of your business,'

Paige replied staunchly. She had too much pride to admit
that it wasn't the truth. Let him think there was someone
else who wanted her...and not for the cold-blooded business reasons he had propounded.

'Rosie is right in a way, you know; you shouldn't
make such radical decisions at the moment. You're still
in shock from your father's death.'

She glanced over at him. 'Is that your way of telling
me that you have changed your mind about us getting
married?'

'No, my...offer still stands.' His voice was low, velvety and seductive.

Paige couldn't find her voice to say anything for just
a moment. She wouldn't have been surprised if he had
come over here to tell her the whole idea was a mistake;
that he hadn't been serious about his proposal. She
shook her head, trying to dismiss the notion that she was
relieved he hadn't changed his mind, trying to clear the
madness of this whole thing from her heart. 'How come
you think it would be a folly for me to rush up to Seattle
while I'm, as you and Rosie like to put it, "not thinking
clearly", but it would be OK for me to rush into a marriage with you?' Her voice was dry.

'I'd rather you made a mistake with me than with
somebody else.' There was a gleam of humour in his
dark eyes, a lopsided tug of a grin on the firm line of
his lips. Something about it made her heart twist painfully. Brad's droll sense of humour had always struck a
chord inside her; she loved that wry glint, the effortless
ease with which he could make her smile back at him.
She fought the impulse now; this was too serious a discussion to laugh away lightly.

'At least you honestly admit it would be a mistake,'
she said with a shake of her head. 'I can't believe you
aren't joking. So you honestly think my options are to

stay here and have you take advantage of me, or go to Seattle and have someone else exploit me?'

'I'm not about to take advantage of you, Paige,' he said slowly. His eyes were perfectly serious now. 'But I can't vouch for the other guy—can you? Who is it, anyway? Not that guy you brought back here in the summer holidays last year?'

'I'm not about to discuss my boyfriends with you.'

'Spoilsport.' He leaned back against the counter top. His eyes lingered on the softness of her lips. 'I suppose what you've got to ask yourself is, do you want to keep your family home or is the guy in Seattle worth giving everything up for?' he drawled lazily.

'Oh, this is ridiculous.' She shook her head. 'I'm not listening to another word. We can't get married; it's preposterous.'

'I think it would be a good deal for the both of us.'

'A good deal!' She was outraged. 'How can you talk about marriage in those terms?'

'If I talked in other terms...talked about love...would you be interested?' he asked calmly, a hint of mocking sarcasm in his voice.

'I'm not interested in any terms.' Her heart slammed against her chest.

'So you are going to run away to Seattle.'

'I'm not running away.' She denied that firmly. 'I'm starting over again.'

'You can start again here,' he said nonchalantly. 'I know how much this place means to you. You can have it all back in twelve months.'

Her skin flared with heat.

'You'll feel a lot better and clearer in twelve months.'

'Or a lot worse.'

'It's a calculated risk. At least you'll have your home back. You can't lose.'

Paige doubted those words very much. 'On the contrary, I think I could lose a great deal. My freedom...my sanity.'

One dark eyebrow lifted at that. 'I don't think living with me will be that bad!' he said dryly.

'That's a matter of opinion.' She glared at him.

'Well, if that's how you feel I'll just ask someone else.'

The audacity of his words made her heart thump wildly. 'Yes, you do that. What about Carolyn?' She flung the words at him, wanting to see his reaction, wanting to know how he felt about Carolyn finishing with him.

'I told you. Carolyn no longer figures in my life at all.'

His words were firm, the darkness of his eyes showing no hint of indecision or emotion on that point.

She pushed a hand through the length of her hair. 'Are you by any chance on the rebound, Brad?'

He looked surprised by the question, then he laughed. 'Certainly not. Carolyn wanted more from me than I was prepared to give.'

Paige thought about that for a moment before she said softly, 'But she finished with you...didn't she?'

'Does it matter who finished with whom?' he countered. He glanced at his watch. 'Look, I haven't come over here to discuss my past affairs. I was wondering if you would have lunch with me? I think it would help if we could sit down and discuss things in a mature manner.'

She shook her head. 'I can't honestly believe that you think we have anything to discuss. You know how I feel about you.'

'You and I have always got on extremely well.'

'Until I found out what you are really like.'

He shrugged. 'I've always thought very highly of you,

Paige. I like your sparky manner...' His eyes slipped down to her figure. 'Among other things.'

'Don't try to flatter me, Brad,' she told him shakily. 'I mean it. I'm not going along with this business deal of yours. I'm a romantic. When I marry, it will be for love, not business.'

'I can send roses,' he said casually.

'It would take more than roses to win me around now,' she said bluntly. 'After the way you treated my father.'

'Let's not go through that again. Your father's problems were of his own making,' he said derisively.

'I'm sure you would like nothing better than for what you did to be forgotten,' she said abrasively. 'But that isn't going to happen. I'll never forget nor forgive how you stabbed my father in the back. He died a broken and bitter man and you contributed to that... I hate you for it—'

'For hell's sake, Paige, grow up.' He cut across her words with contempt. 'Your father was a foolish man; he ruined himself...' He leaned across the table, meeting the fierce glitter of her eyes. 'Shall I tell you why his finances were in such a bad state? Shall I tell you the truth?'

She frowned, her heart thudding overtime. 'What do you mean? I know everything there is to know.'

For the briefest second she saw indecision in his dark eyes. Then he shrugged. 'Your father was weak, Paige, and the sooner you face up to that the better.'

'He didn't have very many good words to say about you either,' she said succinctly. 'He said you were hard and ruthless. And, judging by the offer you are making me, I'd say he was right.'

His eyebrows rose. 'If offering to write off the money still owing to me, offering to rebuild and invest in this vineyard then hand it back to you in twelve months is your opinion of cold and ruthless, then there is no point in us talking any further.' He put his coffee cup down on the table.

'Just tell me this, Brad.' She stopped him as he made to move towards the door. 'How come you can afford to write off my father's loan now and yet when we begged you for some extra time to pay you back you refused flat?'

He stopped and looked at her. 'I had very good reasons for doing what I did, Paige. I'm asking you to take my word for it.'

There was something about his tone that rang with sincerity. She felt confused suddenly.

He saw the shadows in her eyes, the grief, and he moved towards her.

'Don't, Brad.' She moved back from him. 'Don't touch me. I mean it when I say I hate you.'

'No, you don't.' He shook his head. 'You're scared of the future and you are desperately grieving for your father, but you don't hate me.'

'I'm not scared of anything,' she told him staunchly.

His eyes moved gently over her pale skin, the soft, vulnerable curve of her lips. 'I've known you since you were thirteen years of age, Paige Jackson, and I know every expression that flits across that beautiful face almost better than I know my own reflection in the mirror. I know you are hurting now…and I want you to believe that I want to make things better for you.' He touched her face, raising it so she was forced to look up at him. 'I want to kiss those trembling lips and hold you and tell you that you are never going to have to worry about anything again.'

She bit down on her lip. The strange thing was that despite everything she had been telling him she wanted him to kiss her, to hold her. She was so bewildered by the range of emotions inside her that she didn't know what to think any more.

His thumb brushed the softness of her skin. 'I'm sorry I said the things I did about your father, about him being weak. I shouldn't have said anything.'

'No, you shouldn't have.' Her eyes ached suddenly with the effort not to cry.

'I want you to believe me when I say I always liked your father, Paige. I certainly wasn't out to ruin him.'

Paige didn't answer; her heart was beating so fiercely against her chest that she felt sure he would be able to hear it. His closeness was making all sorts of strange emotions surface with an intensity she couldn't stem.

'We won't talk about the past again, all right?' He lowered his voice to a gentle, persuasive tone. 'The future is all that matters now. Let's go out for lunch and discuss it together in a positive manner.'

Paige frowned. What was her future? Leaving everything and everyone she had ever known and loved, and that included Brad Monroe, starting again in a strange town? But if she stayed and married Brad, how would she feel in a year's time when the marriage was over? She would have her home back, but would she really be able to pick up the pieces of her life, forget that she had shared a year with Brad, forget that she had shared his bed and act as if nothing had happened? She didn't think she was capable of that, but then going away seemed an equally harsh solution.

'Say you'll marry me, Paige, and I'll look after you.'

'I don't need looking after,' she said fiercely. 'I can look after myself.'

'OK, say yes and we'll work out the details later.' He grinned at her. Then he leaned down and kissed her.

The sweetness of his lips against hers sent a shock of pleasure spinning deep inside her. She made no attempt to pull away from him; instead, some deeper, stronger instinct seemed to take over and she found herself reaching out, resting her hands against the warmth of his chest. He smelled wonderful—of expensive soap. She could feel the heat of him emanating through her, warming the coldness that had gripped her since her father's death. She closed her eyes and found that she wanted to lean against him weakly, that she wanted just to give in and say, Let's give it a go.

When he pulled back from her she looked up at him, feeling totally dazed. 'Can you hear ringing?' she murmured, feeling disorientated.

He smiled. 'I think you'll find it's your phone.'

'Oh!' She stepped back from him. He sounded so…together, unaffected, and she felt so totally opposite to that, it was embarrassing. With difficulty she gathered herself together and crossed to pick up the phone.

'Paige? It's Ron Harrison here, Brad's estate manager. Sorry to disturb you, but is he there?'

'Yes…yes, he is.' Paige held out the phone to Brad. 'It's for you.'

The slightest touch of his fingers against hers made her pulses start to quicken again.

'Yes?' His voice was brisk. Then he glanced at his watch. 'OK; no, it doesn't matter. I'll come back and deal with it right away.' His tone was businesslike.

He put the receiver down and turned to look at her. 'I'm sorry, Paige, I'll have to skip lunch. Problems at the vineyard.'

'That's OK.' Paige shrugged and felt compelled to try to restore her protective barriers against him. 'I wasn't going to have lunch with you anyway.'

He smiled as if he didn't believe that for a moment, as if he knew darn well he had got under her skin with that kiss. 'We'll have dinner instead,' he asserted. 'I'll pick you up tomorrow night, seven-thirty.'

'I don't think so, Brad.' She sounded as emotionally torn as she felt.

He grinned. 'I won't be late, so make sure you are ready on time.' Then he swung out of the house. Paige watched him strolling towards the car, confident, very self-assured.

Her heart was thumping as if she had been running a race. She was still in love with Brad Monroe; the truth was very stark, very obvious in that moment and she hated herself for it.

This was the man who had betrayed her father, she told herself, but hidden behind the feelings of guilt and disloyalty to her father's memory there was a longing so deep, so intense, she couldn't suppress it.

# CHAPTER THREE

THE scent of roses met Paige as she pushed open her
front door. They were in a glass vase on the hall table,
the tight buds of that morning now unfurled to heavy,
nodding flowers in full glory. She leaned closer and
breathed in their perfume, wondering how Brad had
found a florist that stocked old-fashioned flowers that
still had a scent.

She kicked off her shoes and sighed. She had spent a
dreadful afternoon walking around her property with the
real-estate people, cataloguing everything from the huge
vats in the warehouses to the riding tackle in the now
empty stables.

Everything was listed ready for the brochure and a
date was set for the auction. She wrote the date in her
diary on the hall table now in an attempt to trivialise it
along with a few coffee mornings she already had
planned with Rosie for that week. But it didn't feel un-
important. It felt as if she was writing down the date for
the end of her world.

The knowledge that she didn't *need* to go through
with the sale was reinforced by the scent of the roses
that Brad had sent her this morning. There had been a
card with them, reminding her that he was picking her
up for dinner tonight. As if she could have forgotten!
Even so, she had kidded herself all day that she wasn't
going to go, that she wasn't going to consider his proposal—hence the real-estate people and the practical
way she had been dealing with things.

Her eyes moved from the roses to the grandfather clock.

It was six o' clock. If she was going to have dinner with Brad, then she should go straight upstairs and start to get ready.

She thought about it for just a second then headed for the stairs. Maybe it wouldn't hurt to listen to what Brad had to say, she told herself fiercely.

She showered and styled her hair in record time, then spent ages trying to decide what to wear. She didn't want to look as if she had taken any extra trouble with her appearance, but on the other hand she wanted to look good.

She settled on a white trouser suit and a blue silk blouse. Then surveyed her appearance critically. The outfit complemented her dark colouring, the slender curves of her figure. She would do, she decided. It didn't really matter what she looked like.

The sound of Brad's car pulling up outside made her calm resolve start to falter.

She watched him walking up to the front door from her bedroom window. He looked extremely sophisticated in a classically cut, dark suit. The clothes emphasised the breadth of his shoulders, the darkness of his hair.

She heard the ring of the doorbell, but waited a few minutes. She wasn't going to hurry to let him in… She didn't want to appear too keen.

She took her time going down to the front door, but as soon as she opened it and he smiled warmly at her all her cool thoughts were forgotten.

'You look wonderful,' he said, his eyes moving in a leisurely perusal of her appearance.

'Thank you. And thanks for the roses,' she added.

'My pleasure.' He glanced at his watch. 'Shall we go? I've booked a table at Henry's for eight.'

She tried not to feel impressed by the fact that he was taking her to one of the best restaurants in the area. She nodded. 'I'll just get my bag.'

\*    \*    \*

Surprisingly, Paige felt very relaxed with Brad throughout the meal. The food and the service were excellent and Brad was attentive and amusing. Not once during the main meal did the conversation touch too heavily on personal ground.

'Would you like a dessert and coffee?' Brad asked as he leaned across to refill her wineglass.

'Just a coffee, thanks.' Paige turned from her contemplation of the restaurant to find he was regarding her steadily. The intentness of his gaze flustered her.

'I'm glad you changed your mind about having dinner with me tonight,' he said softly.

'I've enjoyed it,' Paige said truthfully. Then, in case he got the wrong idea, she added hastily, 'This is one of my favourite restaurants but it's ages since I've been here. You have to reserve a table so far in advance that it tends to be a place just for special occasions.'

'I hope this is a special occasion,' Brad said, his eyes lingering on the soft curve of her lips.

There was something so blatantly sensual about the way he was looking at her that she could feel heat rising in waves inside her. 'How did you manage to get a reservation at such short notice?' She tried very hard to keep the conversation on an impersonal level.

He smiled as if he knew exactly what she was doing. 'I can be persuasive when I want something badly enough.'

She looked away from him. 'You mean you bribed them...just like you are trying to bribe me into marriage?'

His eyebrows rose at that. 'I've never bribed anyone in my life. Hell, Paige, I suggested marriage to you because I believe it will be to our mutual benefit. Do you really have such a low opinion of me?'

Their eyes met across the table and her heart thudded unsteadily. 'I don't know what to think any more,' she admitted, regretting her outburst. Brad had been so charming throughout dinner. 'I'm sorry; perhaps the word "bribe" was a bit strong.'

He leaned back in his chair, looking relaxed again. 'Yes—especially for a prospective mayor.' Humour danced in the darkness of his eyes.

Her eyes moved contemplatively over his features. He looked strong and uncompromising, but the impression of strength was one of positive integrity and honour. If it wasn't for the way Brad had behaved towards her father in the last months of his life, she would have had no compunction about believing he was the type of guy you could trust.

'You must be very eager to become mayor if you are prepared to get married in order to secure more votes.'

'It has become very important to me.' He nodded. 'I think I can make a difference around here, make life better.'

'Then what…Washington?' she asked lightly, a smile in her voice.

He laughed. 'Give me a chance. I haven't been elected here yet.' He reached across and poured the last of the wine into her glass.

She shrugged. 'You're ambitious. If things go well for you, I shouldn't think you'll want to stay in such a small pool.'

'This town is my home. Like you, I've been brought up with a healthy respect for the land, for my heritage. I wouldn't give that up lightly.'

Paige thought of his mother. 'No…Elizabeth wouldn't have wanted that.' For a moment her eyes clouded. She still missed Elizabeth.

Brad's eyes met hers. 'She would have approved of my proposing to you, though,' he said with a wry twist of his lips.

Paige smiled. 'Isn't that enough to make you do the

opposite? She always said you were your own man, a free thinker, stubborn as the day is long.'

Brad grinned. 'Funny, she said very similar things about you.'

For a moment they looked at each other and Paige could feel the poignancy of those memories very strongly between them.

'Elizabeth was a lovely person. You must still miss her terribly.'

He inclined his head. 'But life goes on,' he said slowly. 'My mother taught me that lesson when I was very young, and my father had just died. She was very brave and strong and she worked very hard at keeping the vineyard going from success to success.'

Paige nodded. 'She was an extraordinary woman.'

'She used to say, Paige, that the secret of life was not to be afraid of it, but to embrace it firmly.'

Paige's eyes misted with sudden tears.

He reached across and took hold of her hand. 'Marry me, Paige... I need you. I want you.'

She swallowed hard. 'You don't need anyone. You'll walk this election whether you are married or single.'

He smiled. 'It's nice of you to have such faith in me. But I think my chances will be greater with you by my side. What is it they say? Behind every successful man there is a woman?'

'A surprised mother-in-law, I believe, is the other ending to that particular line.' Paige laughed.

'As I never knew your mother I don't know whether she would be surprised or not. But I know my mother would feel nothing but joy, especially if you were my partner.'

'You're not being fair, Brad. You shouldn't bring Elizabeth into this. You know how much I thought of her.'

His lips slanted in a half-smile. 'Listen, I'm so desperate I'd bring a priest in at this moment if I thought it would make a difference to the way you think about me.'

She half laughed at the humorous tone, the sparkle in his eyes. 'This is crazy,' she murmured. 'A marriage of convenience...' She shook her head.

'I think it makes perfect sense.'

'You would.' She bit down on her lip.

'People have been making marriages of convenience since the beginning of time. A lot have been tremendously successful.'

'I'll take your word for it. I can't think of any myself.'

'It's a year out of your life.' He shrugged. 'Then you get your vineyard back... No need to run away—'

'I'm *not* running away.'

'Whatever.' He waved a hand dismissively, then sat back. 'So, what do you say?'

She didn't answer immediately and he reached into the inside pocket of his jacket and brought out a small box. He opened it and a large solitaire diamond ring sparkled invitingly inside.

'You've already bought the ring?' Her eyes flew from the box to his face.

'I feel very confident that this is the right thing to do.'

'I'm sorry, Brad, but I can't say I share that confidence.'

He picked up the ring from the box, holding it between finger and thumb so that it caught the candlelight on the table and reflected a myriad of rainbow colours. 'Tell you what: if it fits the third finger of your left hand perfectly, we'll call it an omen and go ahead... And if it doesn't we'll forget the whole thing.'

Paige frowned. 'That's a bit flip for such an important decision, don't you think?'

He smiled. 'I'm a great believer in fate.' He picked up her hand and slipped the ring in place.

It fitted perfectly. 'Just like Cinderella and the glass slipper,' he said with a twinkle in his eyes as she looked up at him.

'Brad, this is—'

Whatever she had been going to say was cut off by the way he leaned across and kissed her on the lips.

It was just a brief kiss, but it was warm and inviting and it made her forget exactly just what she had been going to say.

She stared at him wordlessly as he sat back in his chair. 'Shall I order some champagne?'

Paige felt out of her depth. If someone had told her even twelve months ago that Brad Monroe would propose to her she wouldn't have believed them, but she would have been ecstatically happy. Now she couldn't get a handle on things…couldn't sort out her feelings at all. Brad didn't love her, she reminded herself fiercely. This was a business deal, nothing more. It would save her home, her land, but could she cope with the emotional side of things? Could she manage a relationship that had a time limit on it, a marriage that she knew for certain would end? Yet the alternative of leaving Brad, of leaving her home suddenly seemed too awful even to contemplate.

'A twelve-month deal…?' She found herself wavering.

He nodded, and with a gleam in his eye he put up a hand to catch the waiter's attention.

Paige watched him and felt somehow as if she had been outmanoeuvred in some way.

Paige's engagement ring flashed fire as she stepped out of her Jeep. Her hand stilled as she locked the driver's door, her eyes on that ring. It was four days since Brad had put it there and she still couldn't believe it. In truth, she was a little afraid of what she had said yes to.

Marriage was one of the biggest steps in life and she had agreed to it as part of a deal. She kept reminding herself that this would save her home, would mean she didn't have to move away, but even so she couldn't help wondering if perhaps she had taken leave of her senses.

She strolled towards the shopping mall, looking smart in a cream suit, her long hair clipped up on top of her head in a sophisticated style. She was meeting Rosie for lunch and she had yet to tell her friend the news. Somehow she hadn't been able to bring herself to mention it when they had spoken on the phone.

The restaurant was inside the shopping complex and it was packed with shoppers and office workers. The smell of freshly baked croissants and coffee mingled with expensive perfumes. Overhead fans gave a cool, restful feeling after the intense heat outside.

Paige glanced over the tables and saw Rosie as she waved to attract Paige's attention.

'Sorry, am I late?' Paige asked as she slipped into the seat opposite her friend.

'No, I'm early.' Rosie handed her the menu. 'But I don't mind telling you I'm starving. I'm determined I'm not going to start eating for two, but the temptation at this moment is overwhelming.'

Paige grinned. 'At least you're not feeling sick.'

Rosie shook her head. 'No, I feel fantastic.'

'You look fantastic,' Paige said honestly. 'Pregnancy is suiting you. How's Mike?'

'As excited as a kid.' Rosie grinned.

The waiter came and took their order.

'So what's new with you?' Rosie asked once they were left alone again. 'Did the real estate set a date for the auction?'

Paige nodded. 'And then I cancelled it.'

Rosie's eyes widened.

'I've decided to get married instead.' Paige made the words sound casual and nonchalant.

'Married!' Rosie had been in the process of putting some sugar in her coffee and the grains spilled all over the table as her hand wavered. 'Did you say married?'

Paige nodded. 'Brad has proposed to me and I have accepted.'

Rosie's eyes went to the ring on her left hand, her eyes so wide now they seemed to have taken over her face. 'I…I can't believe it,' she murmured, totally dazed.

'That makes two of us.' Paige couldn't help laughing.

'Paige, what a lovely ring. Congratulations.' Rosie leaned forward to have a closer look, then glanced at her friend accusingly. 'You never said a word! The other day, when I was talking about Brad splitting up with Carolyn, you acted as if you didn't know any details at all.'

'I didn't…not really.' Paige shrugged. 'This has all happened very fast.'

Rosie sat back and regarded her steadily. 'Did Brad finish with Carolyn for you?'

Paige shook her head. She had no intention of going into the true details of her engagement; Rosie would be horrified by them and she didn't really want to admit to them. But she couldn't lie. 'No, I think it was just as Carolyn told you.'

There was silence for a moment. 'I know what you're thinking,' Paige said wryly. 'Is Brad on the rebound? I asked him that question myself and he assured me he isn't.'

'Maybe he has always been in love with you,' Rosie said brightly. 'You have been away at college for a long time… He could have been waiting for you.'

'You are a romantic.' Paige smiled sadly. Deep down she wished that were the truth. 'No, I don't kid myself that his feelings are that deep and maybe he is on the

rebound,' she said huskily. Then she met Rosie's eyes.
'But I do love him,' she admitted honestly. Even as she
spoke she was surprised by the depth of her feelings.

She had agreed to this marriage because it would save
her home. But she did have feelings for Brad; she
couldn't deny them in her heart no matter what she
might have told him. Her emotions confused the hell out
of her. How could she feel like this about a man she
really didn't know if she could trust? She took a deep
breath. 'I'm just following blind instinct, Rosie, and to
be honest I'm not one hundred per cent sure I'm doing
the right thing.'

'Is anyone ever that sure?' Rosie grinned. 'But I think
you are perfect for each other. He's a wonderful person
and you deserve the best.'

'Thanks.' Paige was touched by her friend's sincerity.

'Are you going to have a big white wedding?'

'I don't think so. Probably something quiet, just a few
close friends. We haven't discussed it.'

'Let's go and look at some wedding dresses after
lunch,' Rosie said excitedly.

'I'm not ready for that,' Paige said, unnerved at the
very thought. 'I'm just getting used to the idea of being
engaged.'

'It's either that or I bore you stiff all afternoon with
baby clothes.'

'I won't be bored,' Paige assured her quickly. 'Anyway, I haven't got time to try wedding dresses on. I've
invited Brad over for dinner tonight, and I've got to shop
for it yet.'

'I'll help,' Rosie said, looking at her watch. 'We've
loads of time for a fashion session.' Then she giggled.
'Hell, Paige, Brad must be head over heels in love with
you if he's going to eat your cooking.'

When Paige arrived back home she was laden with par-
cels and she felt on a complete high. Maybe it was

Rosie's infectious good humour, but surprisingly she had really enjoyed looking at wedding dresses…had got completely carried away with the whole prospect of being Mrs Brad Monroe.

She dumped her groceries in the kitchen then took her other purchases upstairs—a new skirt and top for tonight and some very seductive nightwear for her bottom drawer.

She put everything away then caught sight of her reflection in the mirror. She looked and felt happier than she had in weeks. Maybe this marriage would work, she told herself forcefully. By this time next year Brad might have fallen in love with her…might not want their marriage to end.

She turned to go and have a shower and her gaze fell on a photograph of her father that she had framed and put on her dressing table. The sight of it gave her a hollow feeling in the pit of her stomach and brought reality back with a crash. What on earth was she telling herself? Brad was the man who had ruined her father. How could she trust a man like that, let alone think that she loved him?

# CHAPTER FOUR

IT WAS almost eight o'clock and Paige was in the midst of panic when the front doorbell rang.

She glanced from the bubbling stove towards the clock. If that was Brad then he was half an hour early, she thought with palpitations. She was having second thoughts about inviting him around here tonight anyway, and now here he was and she wasn't ready.

She glanced in the mirror. Her skin was flushed from the heat of the kitchen, but apart from that she looked all right, she told herself as she hurried to open the front door.

Brad held a large bouquet of flowers in his hands. He was dressed casually in a lightweight beige jacket and chinos, but he looked so good that Paige felt her whole body tighten with awareness. 'More flowers!' It was surprising how cool she sounded when inside she was a raging volcano. 'Thank you, Brad.' She took them from him, then found herself getting even more heated as he reached to kiss her. She turned her head and his lips made brief contact with the side of her face.

'Something smells good,' he remarked as he drew back from her. He acted as if he hadn't noticed how she had turned away from him, but she felt it must have been obvious. She felt very tense and unsure about how to act around him.

'Roast lamb. It's not ready yet. You are a little early.' She felt obliged to mention the fact as she remembered the chaos she had left behind in the kitchen.

Brad looked unperturbed by the remark, totally at

ease. 'It's four days since I last saw you; I didn't want to wait another thirty minutes,' he said with a smile.

Paige's eyes moved over him contemplatively. 'Brad, I know I told you I was a romantic at heart, but I do realise that our marriage will be a business arrangement. You don't have to smooth-talk me.' She made to open the door through to the lounge, but he caught hold of her arm.

'Yes, we've made a deal,' he agreed, but his voice wasn't so nonchalant now; it was firm, unyielding. 'And I thought I made it clear to you that part of that deal was for us to have a good relationship. I want our marriage to be as close to the real thing as we can make it.'

She met his gaze unwaveringly. 'But we are not married yet, Brad, and I don't see any point in pretending we have feelings that really aren't there.' It took a lot of self-discipline to say those words to him. She had been thinking very deeply about things as she'd stood preparing dinner. Reminding herself of the fact that Brad's marriage proposal had been made for cold and calculating business reasons. Reminding herself of how badly he had treated her father, and telling herself very sensibly to chase away all the romantic notions that had been clouding her brain, otherwise when their marriage was over in a year's time she would be left heartbroken.

He listened to her as if he was considering her words. Then he just said, 'And I think we should start as we mean to go on.' Before she could move away he pulled her closer and kissed her firmly on the lips. She held herself tense and rigid against him, but as his kiss softened she felt herself responding, yielding to the desire he seemed to be able to stir to life so easily inside her. It maddened and infuriated her, but she just couldn't seem to help herself.

'That's better,' he murmured with some satisfaction

as he released her and moved back. 'Much closer to the real thing.'

'We are making a twelve-month deal, Brad,' she flared heatedly. 'A marriage of convenience. It will never be the real thing.'

He shrugged and a smile curved his lips for just a moment. 'But if the heat of your kiss is anything to go by we could have some fun pretending for twelve months.'

'I don't know if I'm very good at make-believe,' she told him crisply.

'Well, then you had better get plenty of practice in,' he replied swiftly. 'Because there is no point in us going through with this charade if you can't do it convincingly. When you stand next to me on platforms, when people look at us as a couple, I want the body language between us to be right. I want everyone to think we are very much in love.'

'Including Carolyn?' She couldn't resist the quip.

He frowned. 'Carolyn has nothing to do with our agreement.'

She shrugged. 'If you say so, but I can't help feeling that there is a certain amount of male pride involved in all of this. You didn't like being dumped so you are sending out a kind of pay-back message to your ex that you've got someone else and you don't care anyway.'

'The only message I'm interested in sending is the one that counts, the one that will get me voted in as mayor,' he said succinctly. 'And I want to make sure you will play your part. I don't want you to turn your head as I go to kiss you and I want to be able to whisper sweet nothings and smooth-talk you to my heart's content.'

'In other words, you want to live a lie for twelve months.'

'And you want your vineyard back,' he replied, meeting her eyes steadily. 'So don't come all self-righteous and high and mighty with me.'

Her heart thudded erratically against her chest. She could hear it in the silence that ensued between them. She took a deep breath. 'You're right,' she said quietly, wishing she hadn't said those things now. Brad had only just stepped over her threshold and she was arguing with him. It wasn't the right way to handle him, she decided with annoyance; she would be better advised to stay cool. Show as little emotion as possible; that seemed to be the principle by which Brad was dealing with things. It was hard to tell just what he was thinking or how he felt. The dark, handsome features were completely impassive as he stared at her now.

She was very relieved when she heard the ring of the bell on the cooker telling her that their food was ready. 'I had better see to dinner.' She pulled away from him, trying desperately to sound brisk and efficient. 'Make yourself comfortable in the lounge if you want.'

He ignored that completely and followed her through to the kitchen.

He leaned against the doorframe as she peered beneath the pan lids. His presence flustered her.

'Is there anything I can do to help?' he asked casually, as if they were just an ordinary couple, as if the conversation a moment ago had never occurred.

'You could open the wine,' she suggested, desperate to get him to give her some space.

He nodded and turned towards the wine rack to pick out the correct wine for their meal. 'Your own label, I see,' he remarked as he opened the bottle and then poured a little into a crystal glass.

'Good bouquet,' he remarked as he held the glass beneath his nose before sipping it delicately. 'A very palatable little wine...plenty of body.' His eyes moved to Paige and the long pale green skirt and scoop-necked top that highlighted the soft curves of her figure. 'A bit like its owner.'

She tried not to be perturbed by the remark, tried not to think too deeply about anything. 'It's last year's vintage. I've had a few problems since then with the vines.'

'You need help…good staff.' He shrugged. 'Don't worry, I'll sort it out once we are married.'

Paige darted a glance at him.

'We have still got a deal, I take it?' he asked lazily. 'Or have you decided that the pretence is all too much for you?'

'I'm still wearing the ring you gave me, aren't I?' She tried to sound flippant. 'I was just going to tell you that I would like a say in what you do with my vineyard.'

'I thought you might.' His smile was slightly sardonic.

'It's been in my family for generations,' Paige said with a shrug. 'It's important to me.'

'Obviously.' There was a note of mocking irony in his tone. 'I think we've established *how* important it is.'

There was a tense silence for a fraction of a heartbeat before he continued swiftly, 'But don't worry, I'll discuss each stage of the work needed to get the place back to standard.'

Paige turned to face him properly. 'I don't just want you to tell me what you're doing, either,' she said firmly. 'I want to be involved with it.'

'OK.' He shrugged. 'Whatever you want. As long as you keep your side of the bargain.' His eyes slipped over her figure, making her body tense with awareness. 'You look lovely tonight, by the way.'

'Thank you.' She tried to accept the compliment gracefully. 'I just hope you find my cooking as pleasing as my appearance.' She turned quickly as a pan started to boil over. 'If you do, it will be a miracle,' she added with a grin as she looked over at him again. 'Rosie says if you are eating my food it must be love—' As soon as she had uttered the words she felt her whole body burn with mortification... Of all the stupid things to say... Brad wasn't in love with her...had never even pretended to be. 'Well, you know what I mean,' she concluded hurriedly, hoping he would put her high colour down to the heat of the kitchen.

'I know what you mean,' he said nonchalantly, a gleam in his eyes. 'And don't worry, I'm not that interested in your performance in the kitchen... In my opinion it is definitely the second most important room in the house.'

Now her skin felt as if it was on fire. She met his eyes, realising he was teasing her. 'That isn't funny,' she muttered.

'It wasn't meant to be,' he said lightly, and he grinned as he said the words.

She had never been so acutely conscious of a man before. She could feel his eyes on her almost as if he were still touching her.

Somehow she managed to gather her senses enough to see to their meal.

For once everything had gone perfectly and she breathed a sigh of relief as she transferred the food to serving dishes.

The dining room was in darkness except for the flickering glow of the log fire which Paige had lit earlier to counteract the air-conditioned chill of the room. She turned on the lamp on the sideboard as Brad carried the food through for her and put it in the centre of the rosewood table.

'I take it from your earlier remark that you have told Rosie about our wedding plans,' Brad remarked as he held her chair for her before going around to take his seat opposite.

'Today at lunch,' Paige confirmed.

'What did you say?'

Paige glanced over at him, her hand stilling on the cutlery. 'I didn't tell her it was just a business arrangement, if that's what you mean.'

He nodded. 'I know you two are pretty close, but I'm glad you haven't said anything about that... The fewer people who know the better.'

'The truth wouldn't be that good for your image, would it?' Paige murmured.

'Our private life is our own business.' Brad shrugged. 'This meal is delicious, Paige,' he said, changing the subject. 'I thought you said you couldn't cook?'

'It's a very hit-and-miss affair, believe me,' she said wryly.

'Well, you won't need to do any cooking if you don't want to once you move in with me,' Brad said easily. 'I have Mrs O'Brien who comes in every day. She manages the house and does all the cooking.'

Paige's eyebrows lifted. 'You sound as if you have our time together all mapped out. We'll be living at your place, I take it?'

'It would make life easier for me. I have a large office from which to run my campaign and I'll be on hand for my estate manager if there are any problems with the vineyard,' he said nonchalantly. 'But if you'd prefer to be over here, then I'll move everything. Your happiness is important.'

When he said things like that Paige could feel herself melting inside, could feel all the sensible, strong advice she had been giving herself earlier start to fade away. She met the steady darkness of his eyes and found herself remembering the way he had kissed her. She couldn't believe that this man was going to be her husband. That they were discussing where they should live. 'No, it will be easier if I move in with you,' she agreed, content because he had given her a choice.

'I think you'll find it very comfortable.'

'I'm sure I will.' She had no doubt about that. Brad lived in a large residence, a mansion built in the colonial style of years ago. Unlike her home, it spoke of old money and gracious living. It was a while now since she had visited next door, but she knew that inside it was just as perfect as its outward appearance promised. Exquisite antiques, beautiful furnishings.

'So that's settled?'

Paige nodded.

'Good.' He smiled. 'Now...down to dates. I have provisionally booked two seats to Las Vegas for Saturday.'

Paige put down her wineglass and stared at him. 'What for?'

'For us to go and get married, of course.' He laughed.

Paige wondered if she looked as stunned as Rosie had looked this afternoon when she had told her she was getting married. 'Isn't that rather quick?' she murmured.

'Time is marching. The elections are looming.'

'But Las Vegas...?'

'I thought, under the circumstances, that the two of us should just slip quietly away and have our ceremony in private,' Brad said gently. 'That it would be best to keep it low key.'

Paige frowned, thoughts of her afternoon shopping expedition with Rosie surfacing in her mind. Her friend's excited talk about a wedding here in town...who should be on the guest list. The whole conversation had been ludicrous in the circumstances, she knew that, and yet there had been a part of her that had liked the idea.

'We can get married at a chapel down on the Strip. Have a couple of days taking in the sights... Get to know each other a little better.'

'I think we know each other quite well enough,' Paige said quietly.

'Not in the way I'm talking about.'

She felt her heart miss a beat and bounce almost

violently against her ribcage as she realised that he was talking about making love.

His eyes moved contemplatively over the creaminess of her complexion. 'I'm talking about getting to know each other the way honeymoon couples do,' he said gently.

Paige tried not to blush. 'Yes, point taken, Brad. I don't really want to talk about that.'

'Why not?'

He sounded calm and insouciant, a million miles away from the way she felt. 'I would have thought that was obvious, even to the most insensitive of men.'

She noticed that he had finished his meal, so she got eagerly to her feet to start clearing the table, wanting to busy herself, needing to get away from him and collect her thoughts. 'I'll just take these into the kitchen,' she mumbled, not looking directly at Brad as she headed out of the room.

With a feeling of disquiet she noticed that he also got to his feet and followed her out.

'I've got strawberries and cream,' she said brightly as she started to load the dishwasher. 'Or you could just have coffee?' It was a supreme effort to sound normal, as if her anxieties hadn't suddenly raced with undignified speed along the road to their honeymoon bed.

He caught her as she turned and held her arms gently, looking down at her.

'What is it?' She pretended to be unaware of the tension that was coiling between them. The sexual awareness that Brad had stirred up with just the mere mention of getting to know her on honeymoon.

'Are you afraid of giving your body to me?' he asked gently.

'I'm not afraid of anything.' She looked up into the darkness of his eyes. It was a mistake. She felt as if he was looking into her soul. She had always been lost when she looked into Brad's eyes, had always been drawn to them with a fatal kind of attraction.

'I'll look after you, Paige,' he murmured huskily.

She could feel her heart thudding unmercifully against her chest. She moistened her lips as his eyes moved towards them. She couldn't say anything, she couldn't think straight.

He bent his head and kissed her. She returned the kiss, hesitantly at first, and then, as she was drawn into a spiral of sensuality, she responded hungrily, her hands resting against his shoulders. She swayed closer, her breasts touching his chest. Even through the material of her blouse and his shirt she could feel the heat of his body and it aroused her totally.

He touched her face with a gentle caress of his hands. 'I'm looking forward to sharing your bed and, business deal or not, I want it to be an enjoyable experience for us both,' he murmured as he trailed a kiss over her cheek towards the sensitive cords of her neck.

She pulled away, the mention of their deal striking cold through the delicious haze of warmth. She had been responding too readily to him, had for a moment lowered her defences. It was truly alarming how she seemed to have so little control where he was concerned. But she couldn't risk opening her heart to him. He was the enemy, the man who had treated her father so abominably. She mustn't lose sight of that; she must tread warily, keep a tight rein on her pride, her dignity.

'I'll try my best, but I'm not sure that I'm *that* good an actress,' she told him, her voice trembling slightly.

There was a second's silence, a second when Paige wondered if she had just gone too far with that remark.

He tipped her chin upwards and forced her to look into his eyes. Then he merely smiled. 'I think you'll manage OK,' he said lightly.

His calm manner irritated her intensely.

'I'm glad you have such faith in me,' she said crisply, pulling herself away from the touch of his hand. 'I just wish I could say the same about you.'

One dark eyebrow lifted. 'Don't worry, Paige. I think I'm man enough to satisfy you,' he said with a wry twist of his lips. 'Maybe we need to indulge in a little foreplay now, a taster for what is to come?'

She took a step back from him hastily, her blood sizzling through her veins at such an outrageous remark. 'Believe me, I couldn't care less about that side of things,' she assured him quickly. But beneath her embarrassment and her indignation at his words there was a dart of hunger and passion. That feeling disturbed her even more than his words.

'I thought you were worried?' he murmured, a light, teasing note in his voice now.

'The only thing I'm worried about is whether I can trust you to keep your side of our bargain.' She schooled her voice to a low, steady tone with the greatest of difficulty. 'And this has nothing to do with...the bedroom side of things, I can assure you.'

'So what has it to do with?'

Paige had taken almost as much as she could of this rational discussion about such a delicate subject. She was furious that he kept bringing up the fact that he expected her to sleep with him as part of their deal. How on earth could anyone talk about something as intimate as making love in the same breath as business?

'I'm more bothered about what is going to happen at the end of our twelve-month agreement. Will you keep your word and give me back my vineyard with all the debts written off, all the necessary improvements made?'

He frowned. 'You are full of surprises, Paige Jackson. For someone who professes to be a romantic you've got a very mercenary turn of phrase.'

'I'm not a fool, Brad,' she told him coolly.

'I never for one moment thought that you were,' he assured her.

'Then you can't blame me for wondering if I can trust you or not, especially after the way you treated my father.'

'I thought we had agreed to put that behind us, forget about it.' His voice had darkened ominously.

'I didn't agree to any such thing,' she told him quickly. 'I know it would suit you if I could just forget the way you destroyed my father—'

'I didn't destroy Matt.'

'You demanded your loan at the very worst time. It amounts to the same thing.'

Brad swore under his breath. 'You are not going to let this thing go, are you?'

'I'm not going to forget it. I can't.' She forced herself to meet his eyes. 'I think under the circumstances we should have a premarital contract drawn up.' She hadn't planned the words; they just emerged.

Brad regarded her stonily

'I don't want anything more than we agreed,' she said quickly before he had a chance to say anything. 'But having it in black and white will make me feel better.'

'Because you don't trust me.' He said the words heavily.

'After the way you treated my father, do you blame me?'

His features darkened. 'For your information, I've already decided we need a contract. My attorney is drawing one up.'

'Oh!' She didn't know how she felt about that. All right, she had been the one to suggest it but she'd done so in anger, as a way of hitting out at him and letting him know she was no walk-over. The fact that he had already organised one showed just how cool and businesslike he was about this whole thing.

'And if you say "after the way you treated my father" just one more time, Paige, I'm afraid I just might say something I'll later regret.' His words were deeply sardonic, and very caustic.

'What? Such as you're sorry?' she flared. 'What else is there to say?'

There was silence as she turned away from him.

'I have nothing to apologise for.' Brad's voice was grim. 'This is the last time I'm going to tell you that. I don't want you to hurl that accusation at me again.'

'I'm sure you don't—'

'I mean it, Paige.' There was something very ominous about his tone now. It was as if he was hanging onto his control by a thread.

She turned back to look at him. 'I'm sorry, Brad, but I can't promise not to say anything on that subject again. The fact of the matter is, it hurts too much.'

He shook his head. 'No, Paige, the fact of the matter is that your father was master of his own destiny. And the reason I demanded my money back from him was because he was gambling it all away. I was trying to bring him back to his senses, make him realise his responsibilities. It had nothing to do with trying to ruin him, or anything else.'

Paige stared at him. 'What on earth are you talking about? My father didn't gamble.'

'Yes, he did, and very heavily indeed.'

'You're lying!' A cold terror possessed Paige in those few seconds. This couldn't be true. 'You're making this up just to make yourself look better and I think it's diabolical of you, Brad.'

'Paige, I'm not making it up.' Brad's voice became very gentle as he saw how upset she was. He came closer to her. 'I wasn't going to tell you. I didn't want to destroy the way you think about your father and he did ask me not to say anything; he was afraid it would destroy your respect for him. But to be honest, Paige, you left me with very little option. You needed to know. We couldn't go on with all these recriminations. If our time together is going to work, then we do need to trust each other.'

'I don't believe you.' Her voice shook. 'How could you make up something so wicked? I hate you, Brad—'

'Stop it, Paige. You know I wouldn't lie about this; it's too important to you...to us.' His voice was firm, but the hand he put under her chin was tender. 'I'm sorry. I would have given anything not to have to tell you but, honestly, I couldn't go on without clearing the air.'

She stared up at him, her eyes overbright with emotion. Something about the strength of feeling in his tone got through to her. He was telling the truth she realised suddenly. She swallowed hard and tried to blink back her tears.

'Don't think too badly of him, Paige. Your father had problems, yes. But that doesn't mean he didn't love you. He thought the world of you.'

'How could I not know?' she whispered brokenly. 'It makes me feel that I never really knew my father at all.'

Her tears started to fall and he gathered her to him. 'It's all in the past now, Paige. Let's just leave it there.' He stroked her hair gently.

She relaxed against him. Suddenly the pieces of her father's life were falling into place, the reasons behind Brad's actions making sense. She didn't need to pretend to hate him any more. She closed her eyes and breathed in deeply, allowing herself to remember all the warm, wonderful things about Brad Monroe that she had been trying to forget just recently.

'I'm sorry,' she said huskily. 'About the way I accused you of wrecking everything—'

'Forget it. I wish I hadn't had to tell you about Matt.'

He sighed. 'But the situation between us isn't ideal to start with, and I felt I had no other choice but to put things straight. Now we should put the past behind us and pull together. I'm sure if we do we can make our twelve-month arrangement work. After all, it will be to our mutual benefit.'

Paige didn't say anything to that. She pulled away from him and looked up into the darkness of his eyes. She loved him, and she realised forcefully that she didn't want to agree to a twelve-month marriage. She wanted him for keeps.

'I'll bring over the contract as soon as my attorney has finished drawing it up and you can sign it.'

'Yes.' What else could she say? Brad wanted a business deal and if he thought she wanted something more than that he might call the whole thing off.

# CHAPTER FIVE

PAIGE had never felt as nervous in her life as she did when she got on to the plane to fly to Las Vegas. She was to marry Brad at five-thirty that afternoon and she didn't know if she was doing the right thing.

She had spent a sleepless night the night before, tossing and turning. Thinking about their agreement, wondering how she would manage as Mrs Brad Monroe for twelve months. Then telling herself that in all fairness to Brad she shouldn't go through with this, because she knew very well that she couldn't be as cool and objective about separating at the end of their agreement as he wanted.

Paige looked down at the parched red earth of the Nevada desert below and tried to tell herself to be sensible. Real life would never resemble her girlish romantic dreams. She loved Brad, yet to all intents and purposes she was marrying him to save her home. All right, he didn't love her, but at least he wasn't as ruthless as she had feared. He hadn't been her father's enemy. She swallowed hard and tried not to think too deeply about her father; it would only upset her further.

'Won't be long now,' Brad murmured against her ear. 'Then we'll be man and wife.' The words and his closeness caused a tremor of apprehension to race through her.

'All signed and sealed,' she said quietly. 'With a contract to back it up.'

Brad frowned. 'Didn't your attorney reassure you that the contract was all in order?'

'Yes, of course.' Paige forced herself to lighten her

tone. In truth she hadn't got her attorney to check over the contract at all. She had given it a cursory glance and had pushed it to the back of a drawer. But she wasn't going to tell Brad that. Brad had to believe that she was as businesslike as he was.

'Carolyn married Robert Hicks a few days ago,' she remarked suddenly. 'Their wedding picture was in the paper.'

'Yes, I saw it.'

She glanced over at him sharply. Since she had seen that photograph she had been wondering more and more about Brad's feelings for Carolyn. She had looked stunning; Carolyn was an extremely beautiful woman.

'What did you think?' she asked softly.

One dark eyebrow lifted. 'I thought she looked lovely. I wish them all the best.' His voice was flat. 'What else is there to think when you look at a wedding photograph?'

'But it wasn't just any wedding picture,' Paige said firmly. 'It was of your ex-girlfriend, someone you...felt deeply about. I know I would feel sad if the man I loved married someone else.'

'Who have you got in mind?' Brad asked dryly. 'Your student friend?'

'I was speaking hypothetically.'

'I'm sure you were.' Brad sounded sarcastic. 'Well, I'm not worried about Carolyn; she says she's got what she wants.'

'When did she say that?' Paige asked curiously.

He shrugged. 'I saw her a few days ago.'

'Before her wedding?' Paige's heart was drumming very viciously against her chest.

'Yes, the day before her wedding if you really must know.' Brad shook his head impatiently. 'You're very nosy.'

'I'm just making conversation; I couldn't really care

less when you saw her,' Paige said flatly. She hesitated
for a while. She should drop the subject now, she told
herself, and yet she was wild with curiosity—so wild
she couldn't help but ask, 'So what else did she say?'

'She wished us well in our marriage.' Brad didn't
meet her eyes as he spoke; he glanced at his watch.
'We'll be landing soon,' he said, changing the subject.

Paige was suddenly filled with certainty that their
meeting had been filled with emotion. Had he begged
her not to marry Robert? Had he told her the true facts
behind his own engagement?

'Did you tell her that there is nothing between us but
a business arrangement?' Paige couldn't leave the subject. She had never been jealous of anyone in her life,
but she was jealous now. She could feel it gnawing away
at her, and it really hurt.

'No, Paige, I did not.' He met her eyes firmly. 'That
is between you and me, nobody else.'

The seat-belt sign came on as the plane started to bank
ready for its descent into Las Vegas. Looking down from
the plane now, Paige could see houses and swimming
pools and a surprising amount of green grass springing
up alongside the barren ground of the desert. This was
it, they were here... Her heart raced. There was still time
to tell him that she had changed her mind, she told herself sensibly. Marrying someone who didn't love you
was a bad idea... The words vibrated through her with
the heavy drone of the aircraft engine.

They touched smoothly down on the runway.
'Ready?' Brad asked.

No! The word screamed through her, but she just nodded.

When they stepped out of the airport the heat hit her
in a simmering wave, like stepping out into an oven.

They took a limousine to go straight to the hotel.
'You've got a few hours to get yourself ready,' Brad

said nonchalantly. 'I'll have a drink down in the bar and give you some privacy.'

Paige shrugged, trying to act as if she really didn't care, trying to play the whole thing down. 'It won't take me long. I'm just going to wear a suit…nothing special.' In fact, she had agonised over what to wear today. The long white dresses that she and Rosie had looked at had seemed out of keeping with the reality of her marriage so she had dismissed them. The suit had been a compromise; it was attractive but plain, nothing frothy or sentimental about it.

He looked across at her with a frown. 'You should have something special.'

'Something like Carolyn was wearing?' Paige asked, an ache in her heart as she thought about the woman's long white dress. 'I don't think it's necessary, Brad; we're not going to splash our photographs over the local paper.'

He shrugged. 'Why not?' he said. 'People might be interested. After all, I am the prospective mayor. It might be good publicity.'

'Another good career move.' Paige's voice grated rawly.

Brad leaned forward to say something to the driver.

For a while they travelled in silence. Then the car pulled up beside the kerb.

'Are we here?' Paige looked out at the streets with a frown. She had been so lost in her own thoughts, she hadn't noticed where they were.

'Come on.' Brad took her hand and they stepped out into the heat of the day. 'We are going to do some shopping.'

'Brad, I don't want to shop.' She watched the limousine pull away from them with a feeling of dismay. 'My luggage is in that car.'

'Don't worry. The driver will take it on to the hotel

and he will be back for us. Now…' Brad led her firmly up towards the entrance of a shopping mall. 'Let's get you a dress for the ceremony.'

He brought her to a designer shop. 'Choose exactly what you want,' he told her with a smile. 'In fact, choose a few outfits… And don't forget something slinky for the bedroom.'

Her skin burned at those words.

He kissed her firmly on the softness of her lips. 'I'll be back in half an hour to settle the account for you. I expect you to be laden down with bags.'

Before she could argue further, he left her.

Paige wandered through the shop, flicking idly through the racks of clothes. She intended to ignore his instructions and buy nothing.

For a moment she thought about her shopping spree with Rosie and her friend's enthusiasm for the most romantic of dresses. She hadn't even told Rosie about today. She had phoned her friend, but there had been no reply from the house either last night or this morning. Perhaps it was just as well, she told herself now, she didn't think she could have handled Rosie's disappointment along with her own major wedding jitters.

A sales assistant came over asking if she could help and then led the way through a doorway into a room filled with the most exquisite bridal gowns.

'I just want something simple,' Paige murmured, running a hand almost wistfully over a long, antique lace creation. She wouldn't wear anything long or romantic, wouldn't give Brad the opportunity to compare her to Carolyn.

The sales assistant smiled and pulled out an exquisite Irish cream silk dress.

'It's beautiful,' Paige murmured. 'Perhaps I'll just try it on?'

That was it. Once the dress was on, Paige had to have

it. Even if she said it herself, she did look attractive, and that was without her make-up and hair accessories.

Brad came back as the girl was putting it in a bag for her.

'Where's the rest?' he asked, looking at the bag.

'I didn't even need this,' she told him, then felt embarrassed when he asked the sales girl how much he owed her.

'I was going to buy the dress myself,' she murmured, 'but thank you for the thought.'

He laughed. 'Darling Paige, you're going to have to get used to my footing the bills for a while… I am going to be your husband.'

The words 'for a while' weren't lost on her.

They stepped back outside onto the Strip and walked for a few moments along the pavement. The heat was overwhelming. Cool jets of finely vaporised water misted the air as they reached a section designed to reduce the temperature as they walked.

It was the strangest sensation, like walking through a fine mist of rain without getting wet, an illusion of a rainy day in the desert.

They stood there to wait for the limousine to pick them up. Paige lifted her face to the fine steam of water and closed her eyes. The mist of moisture hit against her skin like a gentle whisper of a caress and melted instantly into the sizzling desert air. She thought about her intense feelings of jealousy over Carolyn. It had been crazy to feel like that. Carolyn had married somebody else. She had to look to the future now.

'Paige.' Brad's voice made her open her eyes. He was standing so close, watching her, a gentle expression in the darkness of his eyes as he took in everything about her—the vivid blue of her eyes, the thickness of her dark lashes, the vulnerable, soft curve of her lips.

'I'm glad you agreed to marry me,' he murmured. The

depth of feeling in his voice, the tender way he stroked a finger down the side of her skin before touching his lips to hers took her breath away. In that instant she could almost see love in Brad's eyes, feel it in his kiss. But, like the feel of rain around them, she knew deep down that it was only an illusion.

The car pulled up beside them at the kerb and reluctantly Paige moved away from him.

The hotel was spectacularly luxurious. An oasis of palm trees and waterfalls and everywhere gilded slot machines and gaming tables.

They went straight up to their room, a huge suite on the top floor.

A bouquet of exotic orchids stood on one of the glass-topped tables. Paige walked across to have a closer look as Brad tipped the porter.

There was a card beside them and a long velvet jewellery box.

She fingered the box thoughtfully.

'A little wedding gift,' Brad said, coming to stand next to her. He took the box from her fingers and opened it for her.

Inside there was a stunning necklace made of freshwater pearls and emeralds. 'It's beautiful,' she murmured, overwhelmed.

'It was my mother's. I know she would have wanted you to have it.'

'Thank you.' A feeling of sadness swept over Paige. Lord alone knew what Elizabeth would have made of their twelve-month marriage agreement.

Brad took a step back from her. 'I'll leave you to get ready in peace.'

She stood fingering the necklace for long moments after Brad had left her. The only sound in the room was the gentle hum of the air-conditioning.

Through the open doorway of the suite, Paige could see the large four-poster bed and her heart thudded unsteadily. Could she really go through with this?

She couldn't go back on her word now. The contract was made. All her personal possessions had been moved to Brad's residence. Besides which, if she didn't marry Brad she would lose everything. More important than anything else, she loved Brad, and a year had to be better than nothing at all. She turned decisively to go and prepare herself.

Paige walked through to the bedroom and then on impulse she picked up the internal phone and asked if there was a beautician available to come up and blow dry her hair and apply her make-up. If she was going to go ahead with this wedding then she might as well do it in style.

She had just stepped into her dress when Brad arrived back in the suite. The beautician let him in on her way out; Paige could hear the murmur of their voices.

She ran her eye critically over her appearance in the full length mirror before she went out to meet him.

The dress had very simple lines but it was classically feminine. It fitted in to her slender figure and hugged the curves of her body sensually, stopping just above the knee to show the length of her legs. The beautician had done a fabulous job with her hair and make-up. Her skin had a soft honey glow; her eyes were skilfully highlighted to show their beauty and their colour without being too dark; her lips were a soft peach with just a hint of gloss.

She took a deep breath and stepped out to the other room. The look of approval on Brad's face when he saw her made all the extra time she had spent on her appearance worthwhile.

'You look incredible,' he breathed.

She smiled a trifle shyly. She would have liked to say,

So do you, but she didn't quite have the nerve. He did look wonderful, though. He had showered and changed into a dark suit which complemented the tan of his skin and the intense darkness of his hair. He looked so fantastically attractive... She could hardly believe that this handsome stranger would soon be her husband. Her stomach twisted in a million knots of tension as incredulity and apprehension raced through her.

'Would you fasten my necklace on?' she asked, turning to pick it up from the table.

She held her hair out of the way as he fastened the emerald clasp, the brush of his fingers making her skin tingle with awareness.

'Nervous?' Brad asked as she turned to face him.

'Yes, I am,' she admitted softly, and met his gaze steadily.

'Don't be. Everything will work out fine.' He took her hand in his. When he touched her, when he looked at her like that, she felt sure that he was right.

The wedding ceremony took ten minutes. They had two witnesses who were total strangers to both of them, but somehow it didn't seem to matter. Paige went through the ceremony with a feeling that somehow none of it was real. Afterwards they posed for a couple of wedding photographs and then they went straight back to the hotel.

It wasn't until they strolled into the hotel foyer that the enormity of what she had just done hit her.

She would never forget the feeling inside her. The sound of the slot machines, the buzz of excitement as fortunes hung in the balance.

'I've booked a table in the Oasis Room for dinner. Shall we go straight through?' Brad asked.

She nodded, but it was more to delay the moment

when she went to his bed than anything else. She certainly wasn't hungry.

They walked through the gaming rooms towards the restaurant.

Everywhere she looked people were gambling, earnestly playing at tables and feeding the machines in the hope of winning millions…new cars, new houses. There was an atmosphere of excitement, of fortunes waiting to be made or lost. For a moment she thought about her father and it made her feel incredibly sad.

Brad looked down at her and frowned. 'Are you OK?'

'Yes, of course.' She forced herself to smile at him.

He took his seat opposite her in the private booth of the restaurant.

Afterwards, when she thought about their first dinner as husband and wife, she could hardly remember the details of what they had eaten, even the restaurant itself. All she remembered was Brad.

He ordered champagne, but she hardly drank any of it.

'Here's to you, Mrs Monroe,' he said softly, touching his glass to hers.

'To us,' she whispered as she allowed the frothy liquid to touch her lips.

They lingered for a while after the meal, talking about nothing in particular. Then Brad looked over at her. 'Shall we go upstairs?' he asked softly.

'If you like.' Her heart hammered against her breast.

As the lift carried them smoothly to the top floor, Paige's body was in turmoil. She had never felt so vulnerable in all her life.

Brad inserted the security card in the door, which opened the suite.

He took her hand and led her through to the bedroom. Then he turned her to face him.

'I've…I've never slept with anyone before,' she whispered as he started to unfasten the button that held the silk dress in place.

For a moment his hand stilled. 'Not even that guy you were dating at college?'

She shook her head.

'You're so young.' He stroked a hand down the side of her face in a tender caress.

She heard the troubled note in his voice and frowned. 'I'm twenty-two, Brad. I'm not that young!'

'No. But I suppose the age difference bothers me. I'd feel better about this whole thing if you were more worldly-wise.'

No doubt he'd like her to be sophisticated and knowledgeable like Carolyn, she thought angrily. 'You make me sound like a naive girl. I've had lots of boyfriends,' she told him quickly. 'I've just chosen not to sleep with any of them. I reckon that makes me very worldly-wise indeed. I'm more than a match for you, Brad Monroe.'

'You're probably right.' He smiled at that. 'And I'm not complaining about the fact you're a virgin—quite the opposite, believe me.' His tone was low and seductive as he slid his hands under the silk of her dress, allowing it to slither to the floor so that she was just standing before him in a creamy white camisole and lacy pants.

She moved closer, shielding her body against his, shy and yet so full of longing for him.

'And I feel so much more relaxed knowing you have no one to compare me with.' He smiled teasingly into the deep blue of her eyes.

She couldn't help but laugh and he kissed her again. Then suddenly all humour was gone and this was very serious.

She felt his hands moving against her naked skin as he took off the camisole she was wearing. Then he swung her up into his arms and carried her to the four-poster bed.

She lay back against the satin covers and watched as he unbuttoned his shirt and then started to discard his clothes.

He had a fabulous body. It was strong and lean with wide shoulders tapering to narrow hips.

He joined her on the bed and took her into his arms, running a hand over the satin smoothness of her skin. She shuddered with desire as he touched her breasts, then bent his head to kiss her tenderly.

She returned that kiss, pouring her heart into it, wanting to tell him how deeply she felt about him.

Then suddenly he pulled back from her. 'Before we go any further, Paige... Have you taken any precautions to prevent a pregnancy?' The words stilled her, made her lips tremble to a silence on the words of love she wanted to say. 'We don't want any mistakes...do we? We have to be responsible, especially in light of our twelve-month agreement,' Brad said, looking deep into her eyes. 'If you aren't taking anything, I have—'

'No, it's OK.' She shook her head. 'I did see my doctor before we left.'

He kissed her again.

She felt a tinge of anger that he had chosen such an intimate, sensitive moment to remind her that they would only be together for twelve months. But then of course Brad was a businessman first. While he might desire her, he didn't want her love, he wanted a straightforward deal with no emotional complications. The memory made her heart thump painfully against her ribs.

'Paige?' He lifted his head to look at her as he sensed her withdrawal from him. 'What's wrong?'

'Nothing.' She shook her head. But there was something wrong, very wrong. She had always thought of lovemaking as something special, had never given in to desire with any of her boyfriends because she had always been waiting for that one real love. Now here she was ready to give herself to a man who didn't love her, didn't even pretend to love her.

'I…I guess it's one thing to plan in theory to give your body as part of a business deal and quite another to put the idea into action,' she admitted honestly. After all, he had been blunt when he had spoken about using contraceptives; why shouldn't she tell him exactly how she was feeling?

He pulled back from her again. 'I thought we'd agreed—'

'Yes, yes. We've even signed the small print on the contract.' She cut across his calm, rational speech. 'Unfortunately, I'm just feeling a little bit emotional. I know that's probably not allowed. Did we put anything like that in the contract?' she asked flippantly. 'I can't remember now if I stipulated to you, but I do need to be able to get emotional from time to time.'

His eyes narrowed on her. 'I'll have it inserted in the fine print any time you want,' he murmured lightly, and reached to kiss her again.

She moved away from him. 'This isn't going to work, Brad.' Her voice rose unsteadily.

'Of course it is.' His voice was gentle and teasing. 'I can assure you all my parts are in working order.'

She glared at him, her eyes shimmering. 'You know what I mean.'

'You've just got first-night nerves.' His voice was gentle, understanding. 'They say actors get that all the time.' He stroked a hand down over her face. 'They also say it heightens and improves performance.'

She knew he was just trying to tease her, make her smile so that she would relax, and in ordinary circumstances it probably would have worked. But Paige couldn't relax and there was nothing ordinary about these circumstances.

She reached frantically for her dressing gown, which was on the chair next to the bed, and draped it around herself. 'I think we'll just have to cancel tonight's performance.' She shivered and huddled further into her dressing gown. 'I'm sorry, I know I agreed to... everything,' she murmured, feeling wretched now. 'Perhaps I'm not as worldly-wise as I like to think I am. I didn't plan on feeling like this.'

She glanced up at him, her eyes shimmering with a deep blue, vulnerable light. She was scared of giving herself to him, scared that he would guess how much she loved him and that once she made herself truly Mrs Brad Monroe she would never want to let him go. Twelve months seemed such a short time.

'I won't force myself on you, Paige.' He spoke quietly; there was no anger or reproach in his voice. If anything, there was a hint of regret there. 'Don't look at me like that.'

'Like what?'

'Like I'm the worst kind of monster you've ever met.'

She smiled tremulously. 'I don't think you're a monster.'

'Good.' He reached for her and gathered her into his arms, cradling her gently. 'Because I do care about you, Paige.'

'You do?' She swallowed hard.

'We go back a long, long way. Hell, I couldn't not care. Especially after the way my mother used to talk about you.'

But he didn't care about her in the way she wanted him to. The way he cared about Carolyn. He looked on her as a friend, the girl next door, suitable for his purposes of a partner to stand beside him at the elections. Then, at the end of their year together, she would get her vineyard back, which probably made him feel better because it would have pleased his mother.

Their arrangement suited his purposes. It should have suited her as well. At least she wasn't going to lose her home…just the one person she loved with all her heart, a small voice reminded her treacherously.

'Feel any better?' Brad asked gently. 'I hate to see you upset.'

'I'll be fine.' She got up from the bed, wrapping the silk dressing gown tightly around her body. 'Just give me a few minutes.'

She stared at her reflection in the bathroom mirror. She still had all her make-up on, and thankfully it wasn't smudged. Her eyes were glistening and large in the pallor of her skin, her lips slightly swollen from the heat of their earlier passion. She sighed and turned on the taps to rinse her face and take her make-up off. The cool water helped to calm her. She was going to have to forget what was going to happen in twelve months' time and just take things a day at a time.

When she went through to the bedroom she felt back in control and slightly ashamed of her outburst. Brad had been so gentle…so wonderful today and she had spoilt it all.

Brad had got into bed. The covers were low on his waistline so that all she could see was the powerful breadth of his upper torso, the dark curl of hairs on his chest as the lamplight gleamed softly over him.

His eyes moved over the luxuriant quality of her long hair, the softness of her blue eyes, then moved to the curves of her body, which were barely concealed by the fine white silk. She saw the flare of desire in his eyes and felt her body answering that look, tightening with awareness.

She hesitated by the side of the bed.

'Maybe I should sleep on the settee.' His lips curved

in a rueful smile. 'Only for tonight, mind you. I don't think I can manage much more will-power than that.'

She shook her head. 'No, I made a deal. I'll keep my part of it.'

She untied the belt of her dressing gown, allowing it to fall to the floor.

His eyes moved over her in a studied perusal. She had full breasts that were pert and heavy now with desire. He reached out and put both hands around the narrowness of her waist, spanning it easily, then stroked down over the soft curve of her hips, urging her down towards him so that she lay on top of him, just the thin sheet between their bodies.

She could feel the hard muscles of his body pressed close against hers. It awakened a need in her that was suddenly urgent.

His mouth pressed against hers and they kissed passionately, their tongues entwining, their bodies pulsing, throbbing with heat.

She stared down into his eyes, her hair falling around their faces like a dark curtain. He reached up and laced his hands through her hair, then pulled his fingers through the silky strands, bringing it severely back from her face so that he could see her features unadorned by its softness.

They were so close, their faces just a whisper from each other, their bodies separated only by the sheet. She felt a throbbing ache deep inside to be even closer.

'Tell me you want me,' he murmured huskily. 'Say the words for me.'

She didn't answer him for a moment; her heart was beating so heavily against her chest that it seemed to take her breath from her body.

He rolled her over and dispensed with the sheet. Suddenly her naked skin was pressed against his. The sensation was so utterly sensual that she gasped.

'I won't make you truly mine until you ask me to.' He bent his head and kissed her breast, running his tongue over the sensitised peak, unleashing a need inside her that was so deep it hurt.

Then she felt his fingers running over the flat smoothness of her stomach, reaching down to stroke over the warm, hot core of her womanhood.

'I want you, Brad.' She said the words breathlessly.

He didn't seem to have heard her because he continued just to stroke her, tormentingly tender and seductive, playing a dangerous game of raising her to the heights of ultimate physical passion and then leaving her for a moment to kiss her breasts again, kiss her neck, her ears, her eyes, finally her mouth.

She started to forget everything except the joy of being in his arms.

She realised he was concentrating solely on her pleasure, paying no heed to his own as he stoked her furnace hotter and higher so that finally she was writhing beneath him.

'Please, Brad, I want you inside me.' She whispered the words against his ear and her hands stroked over the powerful, broad contours of his back, scratching slightly as she felt the first thrust of his male domination inside her.

Then he stroked her again, playing with her, toying with her until she longed for him to sate her raging hunger for him.

He came inside her gently at first; then, as she made no cry of pain, he stroked her breast and moved gently in rhythm with her body, drawing her higher and higher until finally he thrust harder and harder.

They soared together in a frenzy of pleasure. When he finally relaxed against her she felt drained with the heat of their passion, but very, very satisfied.

She leaned her head against his chest and closed her

eyes. She was tired. The intense passion, the nervous tension of the day were combining to make it hard for her to stay awake. She wished Brad would whisper just one word of love, even if he didn't mean it.

She tried to stay awake in case he said something, but she was fighting a losing battle and her eyes closed, her body drifting into sleep.

She awoke in the middle of the night with a start. The room was pitch-black, Brad was still holding her firmly against his side, she was cradled almost protectively in the warm curve of his arms. She could hear his breathing, deep and relaxed.

She remembered how she had waited for him to tell her he loved her and felt foolish for a moment. As far as Brad was concerned they had just consummated their business deal. As far as she was concerned she had just gambled her body and her emotions in the hope that he would fall in love with her.

She had twelve months and the clock was ticking.

# CHAPTER SIX

ALTHOUGH it was late in the afternoon the heat was intense. It hung in a haze over the regimented fields of vines, shimmering on the horizon like a wave of molten water.

Paige was wearing a brief pair of shorts and a cropped T-shirt, but she was still hot.

She walked along the rows of trestle tables at the far end of the garden, counting the number of glasses that the staff had laid out.

They were throwing a large benefit party tonight. Almost two hundred guests were expected and, despite the fact that Brad had hired extra staff, Paige had worked hard all day, making sure that all the details were just right.

The band had started to set up their instruments down by the swimming pool and every now and then a few bars of music drifted in the summer air as they did a sound check.

'Paige.' Brad's voice made her straighten and turn. As always, the sight of her husband caused her heartbeats to quicken. Tall and handsome in jeans and a blue shirt, he was striding across to her. 'Are you still working?' he asked.

'Just seeing to a few last-minute details,' she said casually.

'You said that at nine-thirty this morning.'

'There will be a lot of people here tonight, Brad... I've got to make sure it will all run smoothly.' She turned to survey the tables. They had white cloths and pink floral decorations; large silver and pink helium balloons were tied to all the chairs. 'It looks pretty, don't you think?'

'It looks gorgeous, but not as gorgeous as you.' He stood behind her and put his arms around her waist to press a kiss into the side of her neck.

The feeling was sensual and warm and she allowed herself to lean against him for just a moment. A gentle breeze stirred the trees behind them and ruffled the edges of the tablecloths, carrying the scents of lavender and newly mown grass. It was deliciously refreshing and she breathed in, savouring it before the intensity of the heat took over again.

'Where have you been, anyway?'

'Into town on business.'

'Not official business, looking like that,' she smiled. Sometimes she could hardly believe that her husband was mayor. He had been elected just six weeks after they were married, but he was so at home in his jeans, working out in the fields, that she often had to do a double take when he went into his office in town looking sophisticated and debonair.

'No, for once not official business.' He smiled.

Reluctantly she pulled away from him and moved to pick up some napkins that had fallen by the table.

'Why don't you leave all that now? The staff will see to it,' Brad murmured.

'I will. I just want to check that they have put enough wine to chill.'

Brad laughed. 'Paige, we live on a vineyard...wine will never be a problem.'

'It's a problem if it's not the right temperature.' She turned and caught the gleam in his eye and grinned. 'I'll just check the reserves for my own peace of mind.'

'You're a perfectionist,' he said wryly.

'No.' She shook her head. 'I'm just nervous. We've

never thrown anything like this at home before. I want everything to go right.'

He smiled. 'Everything will be fine.' He put an arm around her shoulder. 'But, just to make you feel better, I'll walk with you over to the stock room and we'll check up on the wine together.'

They walked hand in hand down past the pool and out of the white picket gate that led into the vineyard.

'The vines are looking healthy,' Paige remarked happily. 'I went over to my place yesterday afternoon and I couldn't believe the difference over there.'

He glanced down at her. 'Yes, Ron did mention that you'd been over there a lot recently.'

She shrugged. 'I like to be involved. I know Ron is in charge of the place for you, but I don't think he minds my keeping up to date with things.'

'I don't think he minds at all.'

There was a slight edge to Brad's voice for just a moment and she frowned.

'*You* don't mind, do you?'

He shook his head. 'It's what we agreed...isn't it?' He looked down at her. 'I know how important that land is to you, Paige... I take it you are pleased with the improvements over there?'

'It would be hard not to be,' she said with a sigh. She didn't like to be reminded of their agreement; it made a quiver of apprehension stir inside her, disturbing the happiness with which she had felt cocooned since her marriage. 'It all looks so good now.'

'A bit different from how it looked eight months ago,' he acknowledged with a nod.

Eight months, she reflected. Hard to believe that it had been eight months since they had got married. These had been the happiest months of her life. She couldn't imagine being without Brad now, couldn't envisage a life without the warmth of his smile. She halted her thoughts there because suddenly their anniversary seemed so close...too close. And all she could feel was fear when she thought about their agreement to stay together for a mere twelve months.

'Your father would be pleased if he could see his land now.'

'Yes, I reckon he would.'

'And soon it will be all yours again,' Brad murmured.

It was the first time Brad had referred to their contract since their marriage. They had both avoided the subject as if by some unspoken agreement.

Paige felt herself tense up inside. She wanted to say that she didn't care about getting her land back, that her love for him was what mattered... But her pride wouldn't allow her to say those words. Instead she said quietly, 'Four months is a long time.' As if by saying it she could make it so.

He looked down at her and shook his head. 'It isn't really, Paige.'

They reached the long, low buildings at the outer perimeter of the land and Brad opened the door for her.

It was cold inside; the chill of the air seemed to echo the chill inside Paige at those words. Just four months left... Then what would happen? she wondered nervously.

Their footsteps echoed on the stone floor as they walked through the darkly lit room which was lined from ceiling to floor with enormous vats. Neither spoke for a while, and the relaxed atmosphere which had lain between them before felt slightly strained now.

'I suppose we do need to talk about what will happen at the end of our year together,' he said after a moment. His crisp tones rang hollow through the room.

Paige took a deep breath and met the darkness of his eyes. 'Not yet, Brad. I don't want to talk about it until much nearer the time.' She didn't want to face up to reality at all. She realised that was probably wrong of her, but she didn't want to cast a shadow over their time left together. She couldn't bear it if he started to become all businesslike again, perhaps even started to discuss the terms of the contract she had signed.

'If that's what you want,' he said in a low tone.

'I think it would be easier that way.'

His lips twisted in a rueful smile. 'I'm beginning to think there is no easy way to broach this subject.' He unlocked the far door through to the stores and an icy draught whipped around them from the air-conditioning.

She shivered violently and wrapped her hands around her body, rubbing at the gooseflesh that had suddenly sprung to life on her arms.

'Are you cold?' he asked with concern. 'Why don't you wait for me outside? I'll check the stock.'

She nodded. 'I think I will, thanks.'

It was a relief to be out again in the heat of the day, the brightness of the sunshine helping to chase away the cold fear she had felt at Brad's words.

She watched a white butterfly hovering over the blossom that climbed up the side of the rustic brick building. She was a coward, she told herself grimly. She had behaved like a child, running away from the subject that frightened her. But she knew she couldn't avoid the subject much longer. In just four short months their agreement would be at an end, both having fulfilled their obligations. What then? The question drummed through her body along with the bittersweet knowledge that not once in their eight months together had Brad told her he loved her. He was tender, caring and considerate, and even passionate towards her, but he had never said those three little words that she longed to hear with all her heart.

She moved away from the building towards the rows of vines, her eyes moving lazily over the succulent greenness of the leaves against the red of the earth, the plump purple fruit glistening under the heat of the sun.

She wouldn't think about the future, she told herself sternly.

She noticed that someone had left a pair of secateurs in amongst the vines and she walked over to pick them up.

'I wouldn't linger in there, if I were you,' Brad observed as he came back out of the building.

'We've got plenty of time.' She reached to tie up a stray cord from one of the vines, bending to look more closely at the fruit.

The next moment there was a whoosh of water as the sprinkling system was turned on. It jetted straight up at Paige, soaking her.

'I told you.' Brad laughed lazily at her attempts to race out of the water.

'You horror!' she squealed as she reached his side. 'You might have reminded me that the water was due to come on.'

'And spoil the vision of you in a wet T-shirt? No way.'

He laughed heartily as she made to hit him, and instead ended up in his arms.

'You're wicked,' she muttered, but her voice was weak now, weak with the desire that instantly flared the moment he took hold of her.

'And you are beautiful.' He lowered his head and kissed her. For a while all that could be heard was the hiss of the sprinklers and the fizzing sound of the parched earth greedily absorbing the moisture.

Paige couldn't help comparing it with the way she wanted to melt into Brad, greedy for so much more. Everything was going to work out, she told herself dreamily, but then she always felt like that when Brad held her in his arms.

She stepped back reluctantly as he released her. 'I suppose we should go back to the house.'

'I suppose we should,' he agreed, his eyes moving over the firm lines of her body, and the way her top was moulded to the curves of her breasts.

'How's the wine situation?' she asked, trying not to be distracted by the feelings of warmth that rose up instantly in her at the gleam in his eye.

'Everything is under control.'

They were interrupted by the estate manager's car drawing up behind them.

'Sorry to interrupt, Brad, but do you think I could have a word?'

Brad nodded. 'OK, Ron, I'll be with you in a moment.'

'I'll go back to the house and start getting ready,' Paige said with a smile. 'Don't be long. Remember there are nearly two hundred people coming here tonight.'

'As if you'd let me forget.' He grinned and kissed her cheek before striding confidently away from her.

Paige ambled slowly back towards the house.

There was a scorched scent in the air from the water on the arid ground. It hadn't rained for a very long time; if it wasn't for the sprinklers, they would have lost a lot of the vines this year, Paige reflected. And if it wasn't for Brad Monroe she would have lost everything. She should tell him that, but somehow the words always seemed to get stuck in her throat. The result of her own cursed pride...because Brad hadn't said he loved her.

She went up the steps of the house towards the front door. The white veranda was shady, with the scent of honeysuckle; the green shutters and the green cane furniture gave it a tranquil feeling. A black cat was sleeping on one of the rocking chairs and Pip, Brad's black labrador, was stretched out beneath the table. He glanced up as he heard Paige and gave a feeble wag of his tail before going back to sleep.

Paige smiled. If Brad had been with her the dog would have bounded joyfully across to him.

It was cool inside the house. Chandeliers tinkled in the stir of the air-conditioning, and there was a distant sound of music coming from the kitchen.

Paige put her head around the door briefly to check what was going on. The catering staff had arrived and the meat for the barbecue tonight was being delivered. She left them to it, content that Mrs O'Brien had everything under control.

She went upstairs and along towards the bedroom. It was a large room with spectacular views out across the paddocks towards the vineyard and the distant mountains.

The enormous double bed was covered with a satin appliqué quilt in an oriental design, complementing the Chinese carpets, the soft pastel walls and the Chinese furniture.

Paige went straight through to the *en suite* bathroom to strip and get into the shower. She wondered what problem Brad was having to sort out and hoped it wouldn't take him too long.

She was seated at the dressing table, putting the finishing touches to her hair, when Brad walked in. His gaze moved over her, taking in her dark beauty, the way her hair shone silkily as she pulled the brush through its luxuriant length.

She put the brush down and turned to face him. 'Everything OK?'

'Yes, everything's fine,' he said lightly. His eyes moved from her face to where her dressing gown parted slightly, showing the length of her tanned legs. 'What time did you say people will be arriving?'

'About seven.' She turned back to the mirror. 'I collected your blue suit from the cleaner's this morning. It's hanging in the far closet.'

'Thanks.' Instead of going straight to the shower, he sat down on the end of the bed behind her.

She reached for her mascara and applied it deftly to her long lashes.

Brad watched her. He often watched as she put her make-up on. She had grown used to looking up and catching his eye. Sometimes he smiled as if she amused him…entertained him. Sometimes, like now, he seemed deep in thought, withdrawn.

She put her mascara down. 'You are sure everything is all right?'

'I was just wondering if we had some time to spare,' he said huskily.

She saw the flare of desire in his eyes and her heart thundered wildly against her chest. 'Brad all these people are coming… We shouldn't delay.' She started to get up from the dressing table and he reached out a hand to pull her gently until she found herself sitting down beside him on the bed.

'No, let's not delay.' He smiled and his finger moved to the belt of her dressing gown. 'I want you, Paige…I really want you.'

Her body clamoured immediately with an answering need. His hand pushed aside her robe and he touched the smoothness of her naked skin. It was the briefest contact, just the lightest caress as his hand snaked around her back and pulled her close against his body.

'Brad, we should really—'

His lips cut off the rest of her words and involuntarily she found herself kissing him back.

It was always the same. As soon as he touched her, as soon as he kissed her, she was lost…pulled into another world, a world where only her body was in control and her mind was pushed away to another plane.

'You have a beautiful figure.' The words were whispered seductively next to her ear, tickling the sensitive skin, sending a shiver of desire racing through her.

She wound her arms around his neck as he lowered her down so that she was lying on the bed.

Her robe was open; she was naked and trembling under the silky, gentle caress of his hands. His eyes moved over her, taking in every detail. Her breasts were full and heavy in his hands. They hardened instinctively as he bent his head and his lips closed over one rosy nipple. For just a moment she was cool, level-headed, the next she had forgotten everything except her desire for him.

He smiled down at her. 'So, what do you think? Have we got time?'

'Maybe...' Her voice was unsteady.

He took his shirt off as he kissed her, then he pulled away from her to unzip his jeans.

She lay back against the softness of the covers and watched him, her eyes drinking in the powerful physique. He had a body that was perfect. His skin was tanned and satin-smooth. His chest was matted with dark hairs that tickled against her sensitised breasts as he joined her on the deep, deep comfort of the double bed.

His lips found hers again in a kiss that was drugging and intensely pleasurable. Her mouth felt warm and crushed beneath his, her hands moved to trail through the thick darkness of his hair.

He was an expert at pleasing her, at knowing all the things that most turned her on, and he used them with a lazy kind of ease, drawing her higher and higher onto a plateau of thrilling arousal.

She wanted him so much. Wanted him, needed him...loved him.

He kissed her neck then her shoulders and she bit down on her lip as the need to tell him how she felt about him became unbearably intense.

Then he kissed her breasts, finding the rosy hardness of her nipple and sucking on it until her breathing quickened and deepened almost frantically inside her body, before moving down to her stomach.

'Darling…Paige.' He whispered her name as he entered her and she cried out in pleasure, her back arching towards him, her breath shuddering in her body with exquisite ecstasy.

He kissed her lips and she kissed him back, giving herself up to him fiercely, with no holding back. Then together they spiralled towards wave after wave of pleasure.

For a time they lay entwined in each other's arms. This was the moment when Paige felt as if Brad belonged to her, truly belonged. She stroked her hand through his hair and sighed, holding his powerful body close against hers.

'You were wonderful,' he whispered huskily, playfully against her ear. They weren't the words she wanted to hear… They never were.

She could say them, though. Now would be a good time. Brad, I love you… She could hear them inside her head.

'I feel much more relaxed now,' Brad murmured with a sigh. 'But I suppose we should make a move. As you say, we don't want to be late to greet our guests.'

'Yes,' was all she could say. Now she was overwhelmed with doubt, with a feeling that she was the most foolish woman who had ever walked this earth, to love someone who really felt nothing for her but desire.

She pulled her dressing gown up and over her suddenly cold body. She couldn't look at Brad now, couldn't bear it if he guessed at her weakness.

He stood up and walked into the bathroom. A second later she heard the heavy jet of the shower.

Why did she persist with these romantic notions of

Brad falling in love with her? she asked herself caustically. Why did she keep expecting to hear the words? After eight months the dream should be wearing a little thin. He liked her, he respected her, but he would probably never really love her.

'Paige, darling, you'd better get a move on,' Brad said as he came back into the bedroom, a towel slung low around his waist, his powerful body glistening with water, his dark hair slicked back from his face. Paige felt her stomach tighten painfully. She would never give up on the dream, she thought fiercely. Not while they still had time together.

'By the way, I forgot to tell you,' he murmured casually as he went across to open his wardrobe. 'I met Carolyn Hicks in town this morning.'

The nonchalant words made a shiver of apprehension stir through her. 'I thought Carolyn lived in San Francisco since she married Robert?'

'Yes, she does. She is up here visiting friends for a while.'

'I see.'

'I told her she would be welcome if she wanted to come over tonight. You don't mind, do you?'

'Why should I mind?' Paige tried to sound airily indifferent. Yet if she was truthful the thought of Brad's ex-girlfriend coming here did not fill her with enthusiasm. 'Is her husband coming with her?'

'I don't think so.'

'It will be a bit like old times for you, then, won't it?' Paige said flippantly. 'If I'd known, I'd have asked one of my ex-boyfriends over to balance things up.'

He glanced over at her, his eyes narrowed. 'If it bothers you that Carolyn comes here, then I'll ring her and tell her to stay away,' he said brusquely.

'It doesn't bother me; I'm joking.' Paige walked across towards the bathroom.

She leaned back against the door as she closed it behind her, angry with herself. She shouldn't have made a fuss. Carolyn was a married woman and she should be more adult about the situation.

She glanced across at her reflection in the dressing-table mirror. Brad had offered to phone Carolyn... That could only mean he already had her new number here in town...

## CHAPTER SEVEN

THE gentle murmur of conversation filled the heavy heat of the night air. From the dance floor by the pool a band was playing a romantic melody, the strains of which floated out in the still darkness across the open countryside.

Paige was wearing a long white dress of gossamer-fine fabric; it seemed to float with her as she moved gracefully amongst the crowds, circulating and checking that everything was going well.

The faint woody smell of the barbecue mingled with the scent of stock in the borders of the garden.

'Paige, you have done wonderfully well with the organisation for tonight.' Brad's press secretary caught her as she made to move past. He was in his early twenties, tall with dark blond hair and strong features.

'Thank you, Paul.' She smiled at him. 'Have you seen my husband anywhere?'

'No, and I hope not to.' He grinned and slipped a hand around her waist. 'Because I am going to steal you away and have a dance with you.'

Paige laughed. 'Brad won't mind at all,' she assured him, moving to link her arm through his. 'I'm afraid my husband doesn't like to dance.'

'Really? And I thought I'd seen him dancing with someone else tonight,' Paul said nonchalantly.

Paige fought down the impulse to ask who the woman had been and just smiled instead.

The music was slow and melodic as Paul took her into his arms. The lights that had been specially rigged up by the dance floor spangled blue, green and gold over the silver necklace she wore and shimmered over the white dress as she moved. Paul pulled her even closer against his body.

'Now, this is what I call a party,' he murmured against her ear.

Paige smiled, but pulled back a little from him, holding herself away from such intimacy. 'You are an outrageous flirt, Paul,' she told him frankly and he laughed.

'You know me. I can't resist a beautiful woman.'

Paige's gaze moved around the dance floor, unconsciously searching for Brad; she hadn't seen much of him all evening. He wasn't amongst the couples dancing and she moved her eyes to the shadowy figures at the edge of the floor.

She saw Rosie and Mike deep in conversation...but no Brad. She hadn't seen Carolyn Hicks either, but she refused to dwell on the fact that both were seemingly absent; there were too many people milling around the garden for her to be sure who was here and who wasn't.

'You know I've always had a thing for you, Paige,' Paul said now, his hand sliding over the cool, naked skin of her back where her dress plunged daringly and seductively towards her small waist.

'Now then, Paul, not too much of a thing, I hope.' Brad's deep voice from behind took Paige by surprise. It also seemed to fluster Paul momentarily. 'Perhaps now would be a good time for me to cut in and have this dance with my wife.'

Paul stepped back and shrugged his shoulders in good humour. 'How come all the women I fancy are married?'

'I think you like to live dangerously, Paul.' Brad laughed as he took Paige into his arms.

'I can't leave you alone for a second,' he said with a wry grin as he looked down at her.

'Paul is a born flirt,' she told him. 'But I'm well able to handle him.'

'As long as he doesn't handle you, it's OK.' There was a gleam in Brad's eye as he spoke. He was joking, she knew. He wouldn't be jealous; they didn't have that kind of relationship. She supposed in a way they were both free agents. After all, their marriage wasn't real and there was just four months of it left. But, even so, it felt good to hear even a spark of possessiveness in his voice.

'I thought you didn't like to dance?' she queried, slanting a look up at him.

He looked extremely handsome in the dark suit. The white shirt, slightly fluorescent under the lights, contrasted sharply with the darkness of his hair and skin.

'I don't know where you got that idea from.' He smiled. 'I love a good smooch now and then.' He pulled her close in against his body.

Unlike her dance with Paul, she allowed herself to melt in against him and rested her head against his shoulder. His hands touched lightly against the velvet softness of her skin and it made a glow of desire stir instantly to life inside her.

She breathed in the familiar scent of his cologne, and closed her eyes.

'So how do you think the evening is going so far?' she asked him.

'I enjoyed the first part best...' He whispered against her ear, making the sensitive skin at her neck tingle with awareness.

'You have very basic instincts, Brad Monroe,' she said with a smile, knowing full well that he was referring to their lovemaking.

'So do you... It's one of the reasons we get on so well.' His voice was low and huskily playful against her ear now. Although she smiled and knew he was teasing her, she also acknowledged a gleam of truth in the words. They were sexually very compatible, but there was a slight difference in their views on this. For Paige their lovemaking was an expression of her love for him, for Brad it was simply sex. He was a passionate man, very hot-blooded, with a very healthy appetite. Just thinking about it now made her body heat up with latent desire for him.

'I suppose we should mingle with our guests,' Brad said as the music started to change to a more upbeat tempo.

She nodded and was following him off the dance floor when someone else caught hold of her hand. 'Have this dance with me, Paige.'

She glanced around and found herself being swung back around onto the dance floor by Brad's personal secretary, Eric Porter. He was a year younger than Paige and dressed in extremely trendy clothes. Paige had to laugh at the exuberant, energetic way he was getting into the heavy disco beat. Sportingly she joined in for a while, her lithe body swaying in a way that was unconsciously provocative, her long, dark hair swinging silkily over her shoulders as she moved.

When she finally left the dance floor to join Brad, she was laughing and breathless. 'I haven't had such a good time since my student days,' she said. It was just a lighthearted jesting comment, but Brad didn't smile back at her when she met his eyes.

For a moment she thought her remark had upset him, then she noticed that the woman standing next to him was Carolyn Hicks and suddenly she knew why he was displeased; she had obviously interrupted a private discussion.

'Carolyn, hello… I haven't seen you for a long time.' Paige didn't know quite what to say to the woman.

She had always thought that Brad's ex-girlfriend was beautiful, but now she revised that opinion to absolutely stunning. Carolyn looked like a model who had stepped straight from the pages of *Vogue*. She was in her late thirties, with long, blonde hair, and was wearing a black dress that showed off a curvaceous figure to its very best advantage.

Paige felt a momentary dart of panic. Why, she didn't know. Carolyn was Brad's ex-girlfriend. There was nothing between them now; the woman was married to Robert Hicks for heaven's sake, she reminded herself fiercely.

'Lovely to see you, Paige.' Carolyn kissed the air at either side of Paige's cheeks. 'And I don't know about your feeling like a student, but you certainly still look like one.' Carolyn drawled the words in a dryly amused tone. 'Darling Brad, you just robbed the cradle, I'll have you know.'

Paige didn't like the remark. It was all very well for Brad to make dry comments every now and then about their age difference, but she hated hearing it from Carolyn, and she hated the patronising tone even more. 'On the contrary, we are very evenly balanced,' she said swiftly.

'You're not finding life as a politician's wife dry and boring, then? I'd have thought you'd want to be out at discos every night.'

'I have other things to fill my nights, Carolyn,' Paige said with seductive emphasis on the words.

Carolyn's skin flushed as if the words angered her, but she was quick to recover. 'In other words, Brad won't take you dancing. I wouldn't put up with it, Paige. You are only young once.'

'I wouldn't object if Paige wanted to go out to discos every now and then,' Brad said casually.

Paige didn't like the way Brad had worded that sentence. It sounded as if he had no objection to her going out without him. Maybe that was what he had meant? He probably didn't mind. She felt annoyed that he should allow a hint of the fact that they were both free agents to drop in the presence of his ex-girlfriend.

'Just as long as you are free to go off to the opera,' Carolyn laughed. 'I know you so well, Brad.'

They were joined by Rosie and Mike. Paige had never been so relieved to see her friend. With a bit of luck the conversation and Brad's attention would now swing away from Carolyn.

Was she still jealous of Carolyn? she wondered suddenly, not liking the thought but acknowledging that it was a real possibility. Just the very knowledge that she had been Brad's first choice once, that they had been so very close, did bother her.

'If one more person asks me haven't I had my baby yet, I think I'll hit them,' Rosie said laughingly as she came to stand next to Paige. She patted her ample stomach. 'I mean, how insulting can you get? I know I wasn't skinny to start with, but really.'

'You still here, Rosie?' someone said on the way past. 'Isn't it time you had that baby?'

'Our hostess assures me she has hot water and towels on standby,' Rosie said wryly, then rolled her eyes at Paige. 'See what I mean?'

Paige grinned. 'It won't be long now.'

'No... My doctor says that if nothing has happened by Wednesday they are going to take me in and induce me.' Rosie looked worried for a moment, her normal good humour deserting her.

'You'll be fine. It's normal procedure when a baby is overdue,' Mike said gently, putting an arm around her.

'He's read one book and he's an expert already,' Rosie muttered, but the laughter was back in her tone. 'Did I tell you he was reading a baby book? It's driven me absolutely crazy.'

'I reckon I know all there is to know about babies

now,' Mike said with a gleam in his eyes. 'I might even be able to deliver it, if I have to.'

'You can keep away from me,' Rosie assured him dryly. She glanced across at Carolyn as she spoke and Paige could see that she was surprised by her presence. 'Oh, Carolyn... Long time no see.'

'Yes, I'm roughing it up here again for a while,' Carolyn smiled. 'I don't think I'll stay too long. I like living down in San Francisco too much; it's so cosmopolitan.'

'I like San Francisco myself,' Rosie said, but her tone was slightly sarcastic. 'It makes a pleasant change for us simple country folk to go down there now and then.'

Carolyn had the grace to look momentarily discomfited.

'So, is Robert with you?' Rosie asked.

'No. I'm staying with friends.'

'It will be your first wedding anniversary in a few months, won't it?' Rosie continued. 'I remember because you got married just before Paige and Brad.'

'That's right.' Carolyn glanced up at Brad and for just a moment there was a shadowed expression in her eyes. Brad put his hand briefly on her arm. It was just a gentle contact, nothing amorous, and in the crowded conditions of the party no one noticed...except Paige.

'So when is your baby due, Rosie?' Carolyn went on swiftly.

'Last week. We've tried talking him out, but he refuses to come,' Rosie told her.

Carolyn smiled. She had a perfectly lovely smile with small, even white teeth in a face that had a strong classic bone structure with high cheekbones. 'It must be awful,' she murmured. 'I know how I feel when I even put on a few pounds.' She put a hand to the flat line of her stomach.

'I don't think you've ever put on a few pounds in your life,' Brad said with droll amusement.

'Thanks for that, darling.' Carolyn laughed. 'But I can assure you I have. Do you remember that time when you took me to Monterey and we had dinner—?'

'It's very hot out here, isn't it?' Rosie cut in sharply and loudly across the conversation, shutting Carolyn up.

Mike looked instantly panic-stricken. 'Do you feel OK?' he asked his wife. 'You're not starting labour?'

'No, Mike, I'm not.' Rosie laughed and flashed a knowing glance at Paige. 'I'm just hot.'

'OK, if you say so,' her husband muttered in irritation.

It *was* hot, but Paige knew full well that Rosie had deliberately cut across Carolyn before she could start reminiscing about old times with Brad. She smiled at her friend gratefully. 'I'm very hot as well,' she murmured.

They were joined by another group of people and thankfully the conversation moved on to more general topics. Paige didn't think she could have stood listening to Carolyn talking about her dates with Brad.

'Are you OK?' Rosie asked her quietly a little while later.

'Yes, of course. It should be me asking you that,' Paige said cheerfully.

Rosie's eyes moved over her friend. 'You look pale. Don't let Carolyn upset you, will you? She's always been incredibly flirtatious.'

'Oh, I know that.' Paige tried to play down her insecurities about the situation, but her heart missed a beat as she looked across at her husband and the other woman. They did make an attractive couple. Carolyn, blonde and willowy, Brad so dark, his stylish suit doing maximum justice to a powerful physique.

'Besides, she's married now.' Paige didn't know who she was trying to convince, herself or Rosie, and at the back of her mind the knowledge that Brad would be free again in four months was gnawing away at her. He could chase whom he wanted, see whom he wanted.

Mike interrupted them. 'Come on, then, Rosie, we'll get off. You'll be tired.'

Rosie grimaced. 'Honestly, Paige, my husband would have me tucked up with a hot cocoa at eight o'clock in the evening if I let him. He does fuss so these days.'

'Someone has to fuss,' Mike said without repentance. 'You are supposed to be taking it easy and it's nearly midnight now.'

'See what I mean?' Rosie laughed.

Paige smiled. She thought it was adorable the way Mike worried so much about his wife. 'Don't be put off, Mike; you're doing a great job,' she told him. 'I know how wild and outrageous Rosie can be. She'd be out partying until dawn given half a chance.'

'There will be none of that for a while.' Mike grinned. 'I'm going to find an extra-bumpy road to drive home on tonight. I've heard that just might set things in motion.'

The evening seemed very flat after Rosie and Mike had gone. Paige got immersed in a deep conversation with two key members of Brad's staff and when she looked around neither Brad nor Carolyn was anywhere to be seen.

She wandered across to the bar to get herself a glass of orange juice. She felt tired and suddenly a bit light-headed. Probably the heat.

She took her drink and wandered back through the garden. The crowds were dwindling now. The band was playing romantic ballads. Paige stood and watched them for a while, then decided to go back into the house in the hope that the air-conditioned cool of the building would make her feel better.

She chose the path down to the side French doors,

thinking it would be quieter and she could just sit in the lounge undisturbed for a few moments.

She heard Brad's voice before she saw him and something made her stand still.

The path was overshadowed by trees so that the lights from the party filtered through in shadowy patches. She could see the silhouette of Brad's figure, but she couldn't see whom he was talking to.

'It's probably not as bad as you think,' Brad was saying, his voice low and soothing.

'It is, it's all a terrible mess.'

Paige instantly recognised the breathy, tearful voice as belonging to Carolyn and her breath caught painfully in her throat as she watched the woman move into Brad's arms.

'I miss you, Brad... I miss you so much.'

Paige turned and fled back in the other direction, too distraught to watch or listen any further.

# CHAPTER EIGHT

PAIGE stared at her reflection in the bathroom mirror. She looked pale; her eyes, the colour of African violets, seemed to swamp her face.

'The evening was a tremendous success,' Brad said from the bedroom. 'I think we've raised even more money than the charity expected. You did a terrific job, Paige.'

He broke off as she came back into the room, his gaze sweeping over the blue silk nightdress she wore before lingering on her face. 'Are you OK?' he asked suddenly.

'Of course; why shouldn't I be?' She couldn't bear to look at him. She felt angry and hurt...but worst of all she felt as if she had no right to be. Brad had never really been hers in the first place.

She pulled back the covers of the bed and slipped between the sheets.

Brad was getting undressed. She watched him from beneath the darkness of her eyelashes, feigning sleepiness when in fact she felt wide awake.

She didn't know how she had got through the last hour. After seeing Brad and Carolyn together, everything had become hazy. She remembered people talking to her when she'd returned to the party. And then Brad had joined her a little while later without Carolyn. She couldn't get over how cool he had been. Even when she had asked him if Carolyn had gone home, he had just nodded.

He took off his trousers and hung his suit in the wardrobe before taking off his shirt.

'Rosie looked well, I thought,' he said casually, flicking a glance at her.

'Did you...?'

'What do you think she'll have, a boy or a girl?' The bed depressed under his weight as he got in beside her.

He didn't wear any night things, he never did, preferring the feel of the sheets...or, as he had once said, the sensation of her body close to his skin. She shut out those thoughts now very abruptly.

'Paige?' He rolled over on his side to look at her. 'Are you asleep?'

There was a moment's silence before she said, 'I'm thinking.'

'So, what do you say, a boy or a girl?' he asked again, reminding her of his question.

'I don't think it matters,' she said heavily. 'The only thing that's important is that they all love each other.'

There was another moment of silence. 'Yes, I suppose it is.' His voice held an edge of sadness that tore at her heart.

Was he thinking of Carolyn? She squeezed her eyes tightly shut, trying to drum out the emotions that were screaming inside. She should ask him what was going on, but she was afraid.

'I never realised you were such a good dancer until I saw you with Eric tonight,' Brad remarked suddenly. 'It's no wonder that Carolyn was hinting that you might be happier with young men of your own age...going out to discos.'

The very mention of the other woman's name on his lips made her temper flare. 'Is that the excuse we are going to use in four months' time when we split up? That I am happier going out to nightclubs? That I wasn't really cut out for being a mayor's wife anyway?'

'I think you've made a very good mayor's wife,' Brad said quietly. 'And to be honest I haven't thought ahead to what excuses we should be making in four months' time.'

'Really?' Her voice was brittle. 'I thought you were thinking ahead tonight, openly giving me carte blanche to go out to discos every night of the week when we were talking in front of Carolyn earlier.'

'I said I'd no objection to taking you,' Brad said calmly.

'No, you didn't. You said you had no objection to my going.' She turned to look at him. 'It was quite an unnecessary statement, because I never for one moment thought you would object. After all, we don't have a real marriage, do we?'

He didn't answer that and she flared furiously. 'We are free to go and do what we please and pretty soon all the pretence and acting will be over.'

There was a tense pause. 'Thanks for pointing out the terms of our marriage so clearly.' His voice was quiet, his eyes darkened to the deepest midnight-black. 'But there was no need; I do remember our agreement.'

Of course he remembered it. Paige's temper subsided rapidly into sadness. She should be trying to make him forget their contract, not reminding him about it. 'I shouldn't have said that,' she murmured.

'It's the truth. It's how you felt.' For a moment there was a grim note in his voice. 'But you did misunderstand what I was saying tonight. I wasn't giving permission for you to go out as you liked; I would never presume to be so high-handed. I know very well that you are your own person.'

'Yes.' She closed her eyes. She should tell him that the thing that was really upsetting her was seeing Carolyn in his arms. But voicing that made it more real. She didn't want him to tell her he still loved Carolyn. She wanted to think that maybe it was a one-off incident, that Carolyn would be going back to her husband soon.

She wanted still to have some hope that she could fight to keep her marriage. She frowned, wondering how she could still want someone who so obviously didn't love her.

He touched her face gently. 'I just want you to be happy, Paige.'

She opened her eyes and looked into his. She knew in that instant why she still wanted him, why she still loved and needed him. 'I know you do,' she said huskily. And that was the ironic thing: she did know he cared about her; it just wasn't in the way she wanted him to care. It wasn't love.

He trailed his fingers down over her cheek and then curved them at the nape of her neck to pull her closer to kiss her.

Her lips met his, softly and with great uncertainty. She felt her eyes well up with tears as she wondered how much passion had been on his lips when he'd kissed Carolyn tonight.

She squeezed her eyes tightly closed and then, as his kiss started to deepen, she turned abruptly away from him.

'Do you mind if we go to sleep?' she murmured unsteadily. 'I'm very tired.'

'Of course not.' His voice was gentle, but she could hear the note of surprise in it.

For the first time ever they slept apart in the bed. It was probably only by a couple of inches, but to Paige it might as well have been miles.

It was almost dawn when she finally drifted to sleep, and even then her dreams were filled with visions of Carolyn and Brad, their arms entwined around each other. Only in her dreams they both saw her standing, watching, and they just laughed. 'I don't want you, Paige,' Brad said firmly. 'I care about you as a friend...but you've always been my second choice as a wife.'

She awoke with a start. The early morning sun was filtering through the curtains, lighting the room in a warm, golden hue that helped to disperse the cold feelings of her dream.

But even so she didn't feel well. The room seemed to be spinning. If it hadn't been for the fact that she hadn't had any alcohol the night before, she would have thought she had a hangover.

She supposed that it was stress and lack of sleep. She sighed and Brad reached out a hand to touch her softly.

'Are you awake?' he asked.

'Yes.'

He put an arm around her and pulled her close in against the heat of his body. Her body was shivering and he cradled her even closer. 'You're shaking... Are you all right?'

'I think I was having a nightmare,' she said truthfully. Maybe everything about last night was a nightmare, she thought despairingly.

'What about?' he asked softly.

She squeezed her eyes tightly closed. 'I can't remember,' she lied unsteadily.

'Poor baby...' He kissed the side of her neck, his hands stroking over the softness of her skin.

Something inside her just melted. At that moment her love for him was stronger than her pride. She turned and snuggled in against the warmth of his body, breathing in the clean, male scent of his skin.

Brad stroked her hair. The feeling was tender and soothing. She closed her eyes, savouring the moment. Maybe Carolyn would go back to San Francisco, back to her husband, she told herself in a vain attempt to make things better. After all, Carolyn was married and she had said openly that she no longer liked this area.

'Feel better?' Brad asked huskily.

She nodded.

'I've got to get up; I've got a busy day today,' Brad said reluctantly as he let her go.

'What's on the agenda?' She tried very hard to sweep emotion out of her voice, concentrate on the normal, ordinary things of the day ahead.

He hesitated. 'I've got a meeting first thing. It will probably drag on for a few hours.' He pressed a kiss on top of her head and then climbed out of bed.

Paige sat up. She was going to get up with him, but as she pushed back the covers she felt a wave of dizziness.

'Don't get up; it's too early,' Brad said, putting on his dressing gown. 'I'm just going to have a coffee; I'll grab breakfast later today.' He turned and frowned. 'Are you sure you're OK? You've gone very pale.' He came around to her side of the bed, looking down at her with concern.

'Yes, I'm fine,' she lied. 'Just a bit tired, I guess.'

He sat down beside her and put a hand to her forehead. 'You're a bit hot, but you haven't got a temperature. You might be coming down with something.'

Paige felt like saying she was coming down with a bad case of love; she felt hot every time he touched her. It was incredible; she felt lousy, she was torn up with fear and anger about his feelings for Carolyn and yet just the touch of his hand set her pulses racing with latent desire.

'You better take things easy today,' Brad said softly.

'I'll be all right,' she insisted.

He looked at her mock sternly. 'Promise me you are not thinking of going out working in the vineyard?'

Paige smiled. 'No, I'm not. Believe me, that's the last thing I feel like doing.'

He looked at her with an expression of disbelief. 'I

know how damn important that vineyard of yours is to you.' He stroked a tender finger down the side of her face. 'But rest today, OK?' He got up from the bed.

'That vineyard of ours...' she corrected him softly. 'We're still partners, for the time being...remember?'

'I'm not about to forget, Paige.' For a second his eyes were shadowed.

Did he feel tied to her? she wondered suddenly. Was the thought of even four months too long for him?

She watched as he dressed, her eyes meeting his as he pulled on his tie and secured it deftly. Now he was transformed from her husband to a sophisticated businessman; he looked expensive, efficient, incredibly attractive. 'Will you be late tonight?'

'I shouldn't think so.' He picked up his briefcase from beside the dressing table. 'I'm going to make a coffee. Would you like me to bring you one?'

She shook her head, the very thought making her feel ill again.

'OK.' He bent to kiss her. 'I'll ring you later, see how you are.'

The warmth of his kiss made her heart race. She felt so confused. She loved him so much, and yet hated herself for such weakness.

She leaned back against the pillows as he left, then she heard the bang of the front door and the sound of his car pulling away down the drive.

Throwing back the covers on the bed, she started to get up. Immediately a feeling of acute sickness swept over her. Hurriedly she raced for the *en suite* bathroom.

She felt very weak afterwards...weak and tearful.

She switched on the shower and stood under the heavy jet of water, hoping it would make her feel better. Then she dressed in denim shorts and a pale lemon T-shirt and went downstairs.

'Morning, Mrs Monroe.' The housekeeper greeted her

as she came downstairs. 'Would you like some breakfast? I have some waffles and—'

'No... No, thank you. I really couldn't face anything
this morning.'

The woman looked at her curiously, then frowned.
'Are you OK? You look very pale.'

'I do feel a bit delicate,' Paige admitted wryly. 'It's
probably nothing much; I'll be fine later.'

The woman nodded sympathetically. She made to go
back to the kitchen and then turned suddenly. 'By the
way, Mr Monroe's briefcase was on the breakfast bar.
I've put it back in his study for him.'

'Oh...thanks. He left very early this morning. He must
have forgotten it in the rush.' Paige frowned. It wasn't
like Brad to forget things, especially something as important as his briefcase. She hoped he would be able to
get by today without it.

She went through to his study and picked up the
phone on his desk to try to reach him at the office.

The phone was answered almost immediately by Eric,
his personal secretary.

'Hi, Paige,' he said cheerfully. 'I really enjoyed myself last night.'

'Glad to hear it,' she said with a smile as she sat down
in the leather chair behind Brad's desk. 'Brad's left his
briefcase and I was concerned that he might need it for
his meeting this morning,' she told him briskly. 'Can
you page him?'

'Sorry, I'm under strict instructions not to bother Brad
this morning. His meeting isn't until one-thirty this afternoon and he's having the morning off.'

Paige frowned. 'You must have that wrong, Eric. He
left very early; he isn't taking any time off.'

'All I know is that he told me not to disturb him this
morning. That he was switching off his mobile phone

and he was incommunicado, because he had something important to see to.'

'I must have got it wrong,' Paige murmured. 'Thanks anyway, Eric.'

She sat looking at the phone for a long time after she had put it down. If Brad's meeting wasn't until later, why had he rushed off so early?

She snatched up the receiver as the phone rang suddenly, hoping fervently that it would be Brad.

It wasn't; it was Rosie. 'Hi. How are you today?' Paige asked, trying to forget Brad, trying not to think where he might be spending the morning.

Rosie laughed. 'Fed up and suffering acute heartburn. But apart from that I'm wonderful. I was wondering if you'd like to come over and cheer me up.'

'I'd love to.' Paige hesitated. 'The only thing is, I think I might be coming down with something myself. Maybe I'd better not risk seeing you in case it's anything contagious. That would be the last thing you need.'

'Have you got a temperature?'

'No. I've just been very sick.'

Rosie laughed suddenly. 'Hey, you're not in the same boat as me, are you?'

Paige frowned.

'You're not pregnant?' Rosie asked bluntly when she made no reply.

Paige felt her heart flip wildly. 'I couldn't possibly be pregnant,' she murmured in a low tone. 'We are using contraceptives.'

'Nothing is one hundred per cent, you know.' Rosie sounded very cheerful. 'Come over anyway; we can compare symptoms.'

'Rosie, you are making me nervous. I'm not pregnant.' As she spoke, Paige took her desk diary out of the top drawer of the desk to flick back over it. 'I haven't missed...' Her voice trailed off as she saw the dates. 'Well, I'm only a bit late.'

'Perhaps you had better come here via the doctor's surgery,' Rosie said with a gleam of devilment in her voice. 'How late is late?'

'Three weeks.' Paige let out her breath in a trembling sigh. 'Oh, Rosie! I don't know what Brad would say if I was pregnant. I'm sure he wouldn't be pleased.'

'Of course he'd be pleased.' Rosie's voice was suddenly very serious. 'Everything's all right between you, isn't it?'

'Yes...yes, it's fine.' Try as she did, Paige couldn't keep her voice steady. Brad's plans with her certainly did not include a baby!

'Oh, hell, Paige, what's the matter?'

'I...I don't know.' Paige didn't really want to tell anyone about seeing Carolyn in Brad's arms last night, or about their marriage contract; it was all too painful. But she did feel she needed to talk. 'I suppose it was Carolyn coming to the benefit last night,' she admitted slowly. 'I think she's still interested in Brad.'

'Maybe...but Brad isn't interested in her any more.' Rosie sounded very sure.

'No? I can't help thinking that he would never have married me if he could have had Carolyn.'

'You must put thoughts like that straight out of your head,' Rosie said swiftly. 'Brad married you because he loves you. Look how he rushed you off to Vegas. He couldn't wait to get that ring on your finger.'

'Yes.' Paige couldn't bring herself to say that their marriage had been an arrangement, a sham. 'I'm being silly.'

'You know what's wrong with you,' Rosie said solemnly. 'You're pregnant. It can make you very emotional.'

'I can't be.' Paige pulled herself together with diffi-

culty. 'And I want you to forget the very possibility…
For heaven's sake don't mention anything to anyone.'

'You're such a spoilsport— Ow!'

'Rosie, are you all right?'

'Yes…I…' There was complete silence from the other
end of the phone for a moment.

'Rosie?' Paige's voice rose in agitation.

'Yes…yes, I am here. I think I'm starting…' Rosie's
voice was breathless. 'Oh, my God, I think this is it.'

'You're starting with the baby?' Paige stood up from
her chair, she was so taken aback.

'Yes, I think it's the baby.' Rosie half cried, half
laughed. 'I'd better go grab Mike out of the kitchen.'

'Do you need anything? Can I do anything?'

'No, you've done enough. I reckon the shock of your
news has just about sorted me out.'

'Oh, for heaven's sake!' Paige was laughing through
a mist of sudden tears. 'Listen, take care. Ring me when
there's any news.'

'I will… But you get yourself to a doctor. Bye.'

The phone was slammed down. Paige was trembling
with reaction. She hoped everything would be OK.

She smiled. Then her eyes moved down to the diary
open in front of her, and the date. She wouldn't be pregnant, she told herself briskly. She felt better now, not at
all sick.

But she should ring her doctor and go and have herself
checked out. It was either that or wait around and see
what happened, and Paige didn't think she could stand
the uncertainty of that. Trying to act in an efficient, de-
tached way, she found her doctor's number and phoned
to make an appointment for later that day.

Paige went straight to the answering machine when she
came back from her doctor's appointment. There was a
red light flashing on it and, thinking it might be Mike

telling her about the baby, she switched it on eagerly.
Brad's voice filled the room, warm and velvety. 'Hope
you're not out working, and that you feel better now,'
he said. 'I'm real sorry, Paige, but this meeting is drag-
ging on. I'm going to be late home tonight. See you
later, honey.'

Anger flared through her. Brad must think she was
stupid. He couldn't possibly be in the same meeting all
day. Eric must have been right about him having the
morning off. So where had he been?

She glanced at her watch. It was almost six o'clock.
She could try ringing the office again, she might just
catch Eric before he went home. But then she didn't
really want to quiz Brad's secretary for answers. It
would be very demoralising. No, she would wait and ask
him to his face.

She phoned the hospital instead, to see if there was
any news about Rosie, and was told that she was still in
labour.

Paige was in bed when Brad got home. She wasn't
asleep. She had been waiting for him, listening for the
sound of his car and trying not to think where he might
be. But as the illuminated hands of the clock had crept
slowly up towards ten her imagination had started to take
over. Brad could have been with Carolyn this morning
when he said he was at that meeting. They could have
made another liaison for tonight when the afternoon's
work was done.

She didn't know whether to feel fury or relief when
she finally heard his car in the drive.

She heard the front door and then a little while later
their bedroom door opened. He moved quietly across the
room and switched on the lamp at his side of the bed.

Paige turned over and looked at him.

'Sorry, have I woken you?' He was in the process of loosening his tie.

'No. I was awake.' He looked tired, she noticed. 'You're very late.'

'I've had a busy day.' He took off the jacket of his suit. 'How are you feeling?' he asked, his eyes moving over her face in an assessing way. 'You look better.'

His concern irritated her; she felt sure it was phoney. How could he profess to care when he had been out until this hour? When he had lied to her about where he was this morning?

'I feel better. Thanks for your concern.' Her voice was laced with sarcasm.

He frowned and sat down on the bed to look over at her. 'I was worried about you.'

'So worried that you are rolling in here at ten-thirty. I could have been lying here dead by now and you wouldn't care less.'

His lips twitched with a flicker of amusement. 'I'm sure Mrs O'Brien would have informed me of such a drastic change in your condition. And you didn't look *that* bad this morning.'

Fury lashed at her. She longed to wipe that glimmer of amusement from his face. If she told him she had been to the doctor's this afternoon, that he had done some tests to find out whether or not she was pregnant, that might shake him up, that might upset any cosy plans he might be making for himself and Carolyn. The words were poised on her lips. It was only with a supreme effort of self-control that she pulled them back. It wasn't the kind of thing to fling at him in an argument, and besides, she might not be pregnant. The doctor had tried to reassure her, had said if she was taking her pill properly it was unlikely.

'That's if Mrs O'Brien could find you. I rang your office this morning and Eric didn't know where the hell you were,' she said instead. 'He said you were taking the morning off, that your meeting was this afternoon.'

'Yes, Eric did tell me you rang.' Brad sounded totally unconcerned and he still looked amused.

'So where were you?' Paige kept her voice level with difficulty.

Brad stared down at her. 'Why, Paige, you sound like a concerned wife,' he reflected calmly. 'Is this the same woman who told me last night that we have an open marriage?'

She flinched. She supposed she had asked for that. 'We may have an agreement, Brad, but nowhere does it say that I will stand being made a fool of.' Her voice was very cold.

One eyebrow lifted at that. 'What makes you think I'm making a fool of you?'

'You lied to me about where you were going this morning. I felt ridiculous ringing Eric and being told you were having the morning off.'

'Let's get this straight, Paige.' His voice was suddenly very serious. 'Are you worried about where I was? Or are you worried about what people will think and your image as the mayor's wife?'

'I...' She didn't know how to answer that without laying her emotions on the line. She felt her skin heating up. 'I just don't like being lied to,' she said finally.

'Because you don't want to feel foolish.' His voice was heavy for a moment. Then he bent to kick off his shoes. 'Well, rest assured, Paige. Your image is safe. Yes, I was late into the office this morning, but I told everyone that I had been down to San Francisco for talks with the architects about this new development that's being planned for the centre of town.'

'And had you?' She felt breathless with panic.

He turned and looked at her very calmly. 'I remember before we got married you told me you weren't very good at acting, Paige. But I do believe you were being very modest, because sometimes I can almost believe that you really give a damn.'

The shrill ring of the telephone cut the atmosphere between them. Paige reached across and picked up the receiver, her hand none too steady.

'It's a boy, seven pounds ten ounces,' Mike's voice boomed down the line. 'We are going to call him William.'

'Mike, that's wonderful. Congratulations. How's Rosie?'

'Ecstatic... She wants you to come in tomorrow morning to see her.'

'Try keeping me away,' Paige laughed.

'Rosie has had her baby; it's a boy,' Paige told Brad once she had put the phone down. 'They are calling him William. Isn't it wonderful?'

'Yes, it is,' Brad agreed quietly.

For a moment all the tension ebbed away between them. Their eyes met.

'Just for the record, I was in meetings all day.'

She sighed, feeling relieved and then foolish. 'I'm sorry if I went on about where you were,' she said softly. 'It's just that you left your briefcase and I tried to get hold of you to tell you. I wasn't checking up on you or anything.'

'No. I didn't think you would be.' He shook his head and his lips curved in a rueful smile. 'I had transferred the papers I needed from that briefcase to another one.'

She pushed the dark weight of her hair back from her face and sat up a little against the lacy white pillows, holding the cotton sheets across her breast.

'Have you had dinner?' she asked, watching as he took off the rest of his clothes.

He nodded. 'I had something on the way home.'

'On your own?'

He looked around at her. 'With Eric, actually.' He smiled at her. 'He did nothing but talk about you and how lucky I am. I think he might be a little infatuated where you're concerned.'

Paige wasn't interested in Eric, she was just relieved that Brad hadn't had dinner with Carolyn, hadn't seen her today.

Brad's eyes moved over her figure. 'My appetite is running to other things now,' he murmured softly.

He got into bed and his body pressed close against hers, hard, lean muscle moulding to the softness of her curves as he held her tenderly in his arms.

'I think I'll take tomorrow off work,' he murmured as he kissed her. 'We'll go visit Rosie and the baby and then go out to lunch.'

'Will you have time?' She felt a rush of happiness at the prospect.

'I'll make time.'

She snuggled in against him, feeling a lot more relaxed. Maybe Carolyn had gone back to San Francisco and her husband. If so, there might still be a chance for her to work at keeping this marriage.

'We need to talk, Paige.' Brad's voice was suddenly serious as he stopped kissing her and looked into her eyes.

'Talk about what?'

'The future, among other things.'

A pang of unease stole through her body. 'Shall we talk now?'

He kissed her again. 'No, not now. There is a time and place for everything.'

# CHAPTER NINE

PAIGE was alone in the large double bed when she woke up the next morning. Reaching out a hand to Brad's side of the bed, she discovered it was cold. She sat up, and glanced over at the alarm clock. It was almost nine. She had overslept. But then it had been very late before she had gone to sleep last night. After Brad had made love to her she had lain for ages thinking about things, wondering what Brad wanted to talk to her about, worrying about getting her pregnancy test results in the morning.

Her eyes lighted on the phone with a feeling of trepidation. She would have a shower before phoning her doctor, she decided, and pushed back the covers to get out of bed.

She felt very delicate again this morning, but thankfully not sick. Her head felt muzzy. She wondered if it was just stress. She studied her reflection in the bathroom mirror. She looked very pale; her skin was practically ashen, her eyes seemed unnaturally dark. They dominated her face, making her appear waif-like.

She stood under the heavy jet of the shower for a long time, hoping it would make her feel better. Then she dressed in a long blue summery dress and went back out to the bedroom.

She sat down on the edge of the bed and picked up the receiver, feeling incredibly apprehensive. What would she do if she was pregnant? What would Brad say?

It seemed to take for ever before the phone was answered and she was put through to the clinic.

'Yes, Mrs Monroe,' the nurse said brightly. 'We have

your results back. Congratulations, your test was positive.'

'Positive?' Paige repeated numbly. 'You mean I'm pregnant?'

'Yes. Dr Riley wants you to make another appointment to come in and see him at your earliest convenience.'

Paige pushed a trembling hand through her hair. She could hardly think straight.

'Would this morning suit?'

'No. No, make it tomorrow morning,' Paige said slowly. She needed time to get used to the idea. 'Nine-thirty; that's fine.' She put the phone down and immediately felt utterly sick.

Brad came into the bedroom just as she was rinsing her face and trying to pull herself together.

'I thought we'd go into town first, pick up a present for Rosie and the baby on our way to the hospital,' he said through the half-open bathroom door.

'Fine.' Her tone was overly bright as she forced herself to sound all right. 'I'll be out in a moment.'

Her eyes moved over her reflection. She looked even worse than she had first thing. Quickly she applied some make-up to her skin, a hint of blusher to the pallor of her cheeks. Her hand was trembling.

She glared at her reflection now. She looked a little bit better. She just prayed that she could get through a trip to visit Rosie without throwing up on the way. If it had been any other outing she would have made an excuse to get out of going.

'Paige, if you're ready, I'd like to go as soon as possible.'

She'd have to tell Brad. She closed her eyes, weak with panic at the thought. She couldn't face that yet.

'I'm ready.' She strode out into the bedroom and deliberately didn't meet his gaze. 'I'll just get my hand-bag.'

Brad slanted a curious glance at her as they went outside to the car. 'Did you sleep OK last night?'

Paige nodded and got gratefully into the car as he pressed the central-locking switch.

As they drove she looked out at the passing scenery. The sky was blue, without a cloud in sight. The fields looked lush and inviting. What was she going to do? she wondered.

'Do you think Carolyn will stay in town for long?' she asked suddenly.

'I think she will be here for a while.' Brad's voice lowered. 'Between you and me, Paige, Carolyn's marriage has broken up.'

Brad flicked a glance at her as she made no reply. 'She's had a pretty tough time of it lately...'

The compassion in Brad's tone tore at Paige.

'Poor Carolyn.' It was all she could say; her voice was raw.

Judging by what he had just said and what she had witnessed the other night, it sounded as if they might want to get back together. She did, after all, have no real hold on him, she reminded herself.

Where the hell did that leave her? she wondered, and she felt an unbearable wedge of anguish settle inside her.

She was going to have to be cool and collected and think rationally about what she should do. She only hoped that Rosie wouldn't say anything about her being pregnant when they saw her in hospital... She couldn't cope with Brad knowing the truth...not until she had sorted out her own feelings.

'Congratulations.' Paige bent to kiss her friend's cheek. 'How are you feeling?'

'I feel like the happiest person alive,' Rosie said sincerely.

She was sitting up in bed, wearing a pink nightgown, her face shining with animated joy. Mike had risen from the chair beside her bed as they'd walked into the room and he stood beside her now, beaming down at his wife.

'She was very brave,' he said softly.

'Was it very painful?' Paige asked with a grimace. 'You did seem to be in labour a long time.'

'There was a lot of screaming, believe me,' Mike said wryly.

'And that was just Mike...' Rosie laughed cheerfully. 'Don't be put off by him, Paige; it wasn't that bad.'

Brad reached down to kiss her on the cheek and then shook Mike warmly by the hand as Paige moved to look down into the crib. 'Hello, William,' she said softly, putting down a hand to move the cotton blanket.

He was tiny, with a shock of dark hair and the largest blue eyes, which seemed to look up at Paige as if he recognised her. He smiled up at her and gurgled happily.

'He's gorgeous, Rosie; you're so lucky.'

'I know.' Rosie leaned across to look in at her son. 'Worth every bit of the pain, Paige, believe me,' she said dreamily.

Paige smiled.

'Pick him up if you like,' Rosie urged.

Paige hesitated for a second, then reached into the cot.

The little body was warm in her arms. He lay looking up at her with such trust, such innocence that she felt quite overwhelmed by him.

She sat back in the chair which Mike had occupied just a few moments before and rocked the baby gently in her arms, studying the small hands, the pinkness of his skin, the surprising darkness of his hair and eyelashes.

'Feels good, doesn't it?' Rosie said with a smile.

'Yes...he's wonderful.' Paige felt her emotions like molten lava inside her, the feelings of tenderness for the baby making her so aware that she desperately wanted Brad's child. But she had to be realistic. She could be left alone to bring up the baby and how would she cope? But worse, she didn't want Brad to feel trapped into staying with her if he didn't want to. He could end up hating her. She remembered how he had told her that children weren't part of their deal when he had proposed to her.

She looked up and found her husband's eyes resting on her contemplatively, taking in the gentle way she was holding the baby, the bright sparkle in her eyes.

'It was good of you to take the time to come in and see us, Brad,' Mike said now. 'I bet it's not every day that a baby gets a visit from the mayor of the town.'

'Oh, you'd be surprised. I do get around the hospital wards from time to time.' Brad grinned and walked over to have a closer look at the baby.

'Do you want to hold him?' Rosie asked.

Paige was surprised when Brad reached down and willingly took the child from her.

His hands looked so large against the tiny baby. He cradled him gently, looking quite at ease with him.

'A born father,' Rosie grinned. 'It will be your turn next, Brad.'

Paige felt her stomach muscles contract as she looked up and met Brad's eyes. It was hard to tell what he made of that remark; the dark eyes were unfathomable. Probably thinking that if he was to become a father it wouldn't be with her as a partner, Paige thought suddenly, her hands clenching tightly as they rested on her lap.

'What do you say, Paige?' Paige was very aware of Rosie's probing eyes on her.

'I don't think so, Rosie,' she said coolly. 'Fatherhood

wouldn't suit Brad at all. It would get in the way of more urgent plans.'

There was a moment's strained silence and Paige saw Brad's features tighten imperceptibly before he looked away from her.

The conversation flowed over Paige's head for a moment. She found herself regretting her words as she watched the way Brad was still holding the baby, the soothing way he was rocking the child as he talked. She had been totally out of order, she knew that. Brad would probably make a terrific father...with the right woman by his side. Her eyes were shadowed with sadness as she looked back at Rosie.

'So, no news, then?' she asked softly.

Paige knew very well that she was asking if she was pregnant. She felt a wave of hot colour in her face as she met Rosie's eyes. 'Only the prospect of a business dinner tomorrow night,' she said uncomfortably.

Brad handed William back to her. 'I suppose we should be going.'

Rosie smiled. 'Heavy day ahead?' she asked him.

He shook his head. 'Only in so far as I am entertaining my wife today.' He grinned across at Paige. 'I booked a table at Henry's.'

Paige's thoughts had been so taken up by the news of her pregnancy that she had forgotten that he had said he was taking her for lunch. She hoped she would be able to eat something. 'That's where we got engaged,' she reflected. 'Do you remember?'

'Of course I remember.' He smiled.

'Sounds romantic,' Rosie said.

Paige looked over at Brad. She really hoped so. Heavens, she would give her soul for Brad to turn around and tell her he loved her...that he didn't want their relationship to end.

*     *     *

'So what would you like?' Brad asked as the waitress came across to take their order.

She glanced down at the menu, her eyes flitting over the garlic dishes as her stomach reminded her tenderly that she was only just starting to feel better.

'I'll have a garden salad and the chef's special, please,' she said decisively, closing the menu again.

Brad started to order wine, and she cut across him. 'Just water for me, Brad.'

'Are you sure that was all you wanted?' Brad asked as the waitress left them. 'Are you still not feeling well?'

'I'm fine...really.' She looked around the restaurant. It was stylish and relaxed. In the far corner a couple were dining with their two children, two very pretty little girls of about nine years of age. For some reason the happy family scene made her want to cry suddenly.

She returned her attention to the table and found that Brad was looking at her with almost the same amount of concentration that she had been giving to their surroundings.

She was glad that she had gone to a lot of trouble with her appearance. Her dark hair was smoothly perfect, her make-up light yet subtle enough to give a hint of a peach blush to the translucent quality of her skin, her only jewellery the gold band of her wedding ring.

His gaze lingered for a moment on that ring.

'Hard to believe that we've been married for eight months.'

'Yes.' She looked away from him and unconsciously she twisted her wedding ring around and around.

'You know we are going to have to start making decisions about what we're going to do when it comes up to our anniversary.'

'Yes, I know.' She took a deep breath. She was going to have to face this subject sooner or later, but she didn't

know if she had the strength today. 'Is that the reason
you suggested lunch today?'

He shrugged. 'Not entirely. I just thought it would be
a good chance for us to talk…' He grinned suddenly.
'Let's face it…a conversation when we are in bed can
be a bit distracting.' His eyes moved very briefly over
the soft curves of her figure, making her blush. 'And it's
good for us to get out together, away from the phones
and the constant interruptions.'

Just as he spoke his mobile phone rang. 'Hell's bells,
I thought I'd switched that thing off.' He grinned rue-
fully over at her as he reached to take the offending item
from his jacket.

'Yes… No. I can't talk now. I'll come over later.' He
switched the phone off and put it away. 'Sorry about
that, Paige.'

'That's OK.' She couldn't help wondering if that had
been Carolyn. She swept the unsavoury thought immediately away. But her skin was pale now, her eyes a deep
shade of blue as she looked across at him.

'Who was that?'

'Just the office.' His gaze lingered on the soft, vulnerable curve of her lips. 'As I was saying, I think we
need to take some time just for us…time to really sit
down and work out what we want to do.'

'Yes.' Her heart was slamming against her chest and
she felt a bit light-headed for a moment.

'Are you OK?' He frowned.

'I…I feel a bit tense about the subject,' she admitted
wryly. 'But I know you're right; we've got to start sorting out what will happen in four months.' She shrugged
helplessly. 'I'm feeling a bit under the weather at the
moment…' She tried to make excuses for the fact that
she knew she looked stressed. Knew that her emotions
were balanced very precariously.

There was a look of concern on his face. 'You've had

a lot on your plate recently…helping me, sorting all the details for that benefit.' He sighed. 'I'm sure there have been moments recently when you have wondered what the hell you've taken on with me—'

'I'm not an empty-headed little girl, Brad, who expects just to sit back and be entertained, you know…' She cut across him tetchily. 'I have enjoyed working alongside you.'

'Hell, Paige, I know that and I'm not complaining for one moment about the way you've stood by me since we got married.' He looked across at her earnestly. 'And I appreciate it, I really do. I suppose I'm saying that there is a part of me that still feels guilty for…coercing you into this situation. You say you knew what you were doing when you agreed to our marriage…but in truth it was a very emotional time for you. You were torn by grief—'

'Feeling like that, I'm surprised you even considered asking me to marry you…whether out of business reasons or any other,' she muttered.

'Believe it or not, that night when I came over to the vineyard to see how you were, I hadn't planned to ask you to marry me.' He reached out a hand and covered hers as it rested on the tablecloth. 'I just looked into your eyes and it happened.' His lips curved in a crooked smile. 'I guess you could say it was a moment of weakness on my part. I'd told myself that you were not for me…that you were far too young. Then all of a sudden I was thinking, What the heck? Let's give it a go.'

Paige didn't say anything. She knew very well that it had been a moment of weakness on his part. He had been on the rebound from Carolyn. She had always known it. And now Carolyn was back and available.

'Is this your prelude to saying maybe it's as well we are coming up to a parting of the ways?' she asked him bluntly.

'Of course not; it's a prelude to saying our anniversary is coming up and we need to sit down sensibly and discuss things.'

'So here we are at Henry's—a kind of revisit to the scene of our engagement...sorry, the birth of our business deal. So that we can say, "Hey, we've almost come full circle now; let's start talking about splitting up."'

'I wasn't going to put it quite as bluntly as that.' His voice grated rawly. 'I don't think we need to make any hasty decisions. I know we made an agreement for twelve months, Paige, but I had no intention of just turning around to you at the end of that time and saying, "Right, bye, see you around."'

Her heart bounced painfully in her chest. No, he wouldn't, she realised. Brad was too much of a gentleman for that. He had been kind and considerate to her during their time together, had made love to her with warmth and tenderness. He would never just turn around and say, "Here's your property back; thanks for the memories." He would discuss things; he would be gentle. He would never want to hurt her; he probably felt too much of a sense of responsibility for her. To him she was still the young girl whom his mother had adored. He wouldn't just abandon her.

She closed her eyes on a wealth of sadness. And if she told him she was pregnant he certainly wouldn't walk away from her.

But she didn't want his kindness, his sympathy; she wanted his love.

'Paige?'

His voice, gently probing, made her take a deep breath.

'I guess what I'm saying is that you mustn't feel you've got to end things in four months. In fact, I think you should stay on for a while—'

'Yes, OK, Brad, I get the picture.' She cut across him hurriedly. 'I'll think about it.'

He looked tense. She could see a muscle pulsing at the side of his forehead and his eyes were bleak as they met hers.

'Let's not talk about the future any more,' she said grimly. 'To be honest, it's as much as I can do to get through a day at a time.'

'Are you so unhappy?' He frowned. 'Until just recently I thought that things were working out fine.'

'They were... They are.' She shook her head. 'And I appreciate everything you've done for me, Brad. The way you've turned the vineyard around, the time and the effort you've put into restoring my house, my land—'

'For hell's sake, Paige, I don't want your gratitude.' He interrupted her angrily. 'I told you I'd do that.'

'Yes, I know, we had an agreement.' She nodded. 'But you didn't have to do all that for me...spend all that money bailing me out, helping me.' She met his eyes steadily across the table. 'I realise it was part of the deal, but even so you have been exceptionally generous.'

He opened his mouth to say something but she continued swiftly. 'I've been meaning to say thank you for a very long time,' she said softly.

'You don't need to say it.' His voice was heavy.

'I think I do.' She looked over at him steadily. 'I feel awful sometimes when I think about the way I accused you over my father's financial problems.'

He shrugged. 'I wish I hadn't had to tell you the truth. I would have liked to have spared you that.'

Their meal arrived and for a while there was silence between them.

Brad was a decent and honourable man...she knew that. Just as she knew that he believed she was just as focused on the business side of their relationship as he was. He would be horrified if he knew how upset she was at the thought of losing him. And he would be consumed with guilt if he knew she was expecting his child.

He cared about her as a friend, and as he saw things he had genuinely tried to help her when he'd married her.

When he had proposed he had already lost the one woman he loved, and she supposed he had felt he had very little to lose and everything to gain by their marriage, as it had helped secure his mayorship. He would see this situation as very satisfactory. They both had what they wanted. They could part amicably, in a civilised fashion, with no recriminations. He could even pick up where he'd left off with Carolyn, without a need to feel in the slightest bit guilty.

The news of her pregnancy would be a bombshell. She couldn't face telling him.

She picked at the food in front of her. She really didn't feel at all well.

'It's nearly a year since your father died, isn't it?' Brad said suddenly. 'Do you think that's why you're feeling a bit tense at the moment...a bit sad?'

'Possibly.' She took a deep breath, then grasped the excuse to get out of any further discussion about the end of their agreement. 'So let's just talk about happy things, shall we? And leave all that other emotional stuff for another few months.'

He hesitated. 'Whatever you want, Paige, is fine by me.'

# CHAPTER TEN

PAIGE sat on the veranda of her old home, her eyes sweeping over the countryside as she sipped a cool glass of lemonade.

The fields of vines shimmered in the sunshine, a small breeze rustling the leaves with a whispering, tranquil sound.

She was going to have a baby... She kept saying it to herself. Then she put a hand down on the flat line of her stomach.

Ten weeks pregnant...and still Brad didn't know. She had told Rosie but not her own husband. There was a curl of guilt there, mixed with an almighty amount of trepidation.

She really was going to have to tell Brad, but when? The date of their anniversary was looming ever closer. Just nine weeks now. Her heart thudded erratically at the very thought.

She heard the distant sound of a car and looked over towards the driveway as Brad's bright red Porsche pulled in.

'Ron said I'd find you here,' he said as he got out.

He was dressed in jeans and a lightweight blue shirt. Her eyes moved over him, taking in every detail of his tall, powerful frame as he held the door for his black labrador, Pip, to jump out behind him.

'I saw Ron a little while ago,' Paige said with a nod. She glanced at her watch. 'You've finished work early. I thought you'd be at the office until at least six.'

'I'd had enough by four.' He grinned at her as he sat down beside her on the step.

Pip sat next to him and rested his head on Brad's denim knee, looking at Paige with big, soulful brown eyes.

She stretched out a hand to stroke him.

'So what are you doing up here?' Brad asked briskly.

'Just relaxing…thinking.' She shrugged.

'Thinking about that letter you received this morning?' he asked nonchalantly.

'What letter?' She was momentarily surprised by the question.

'The one from your ex-boyfriend. What was his name…?'

'Josh.' She nodded. She had forgotten she had received a letter from him this morning. It had been readdressed via the postal service from this address. 'How did you know it was from him?'

'I noticed his name and address on the back of the envelope when I brought it into the study.' He smiled. 'I'd make a great detective, don't you think?'

'Probably.' She smiled.

'So what did he want?'

'Just telling me that I'd always be welcome to go up and see him. He's got a good job. His sister is getting married.' She shrugged. 'Just a chatty, newsy letter, nothing special.'

'And are you going to go?'

The question startled her. She hadn't even given Josh's invitation a second thought. Did Brad want her to go? she wondered suddenly. Was he thinking it would make their split easier if she had someone else? Make him able to turn completely to Carolyn without worrying about her?

'I…I shouldn't think so.' It took all her strength to keep the tremble of emotion out of her voice. She had managed to put Carolyn out of her mind over these last few weeks; her thoughts had been centred on her baby, her future. She didn't want to start thinking about Carolyn and Brad; it would just drive her crazy.

Brad glanced over at her and his eyes narrowed on the over-bright sparkle in her eyes.

'It's too hot out here for Pip.' Paige changed the conversation abruptly, her fingers running soothingly over the dog's glossy coat. He was panting; the heat did not suit him.

'Poor old Pip.' Brad's voice made the animal prick up his ears. 'Come on, let's get you a drink.' Brad stood up and the dog followed him obediently into the house.

When he came back, Paige had composed herself a little.

Brad sat back on the step and Pip flopped down further behind them in the shade.

'I don't know what to wear to this party tonight,' she murmured. In truth, she wasn't looking forward to going out tonight. She still wasn't feeling one hundred per cent.

'I'll take you into town and buy you a new dress if you like.' He glanced at his watch. 'We've got time.'

She smiled at him. 'That's a nice thought... Thanks. But I'll have a root through the closet, see what I can find.'

He shrugged. 'You'll look good no matter what, but I just thought it might make you feel better.'

She looked over at him with a raised eyebrow.

He shrugged again. 'I couldn't help noticing that you looked upset a moment ago when we spoke about Josh.'

'I didn't look upset; that's your imagination,' she said quickly.

'Not dwelling on what might have been, are you?' he asked lightly. 'He did once ask you to move in with him, share his apartment, didn't he?'

Paige smiled. 'I never said that.'

'I thought you did,' Brad said. 'I seem to remember

something about it... Anyway I think you did the right thing staying here.'

'Why do you say that?' She turned and batted wide eyes at him.

'Because I'm a much better catch, of course.' There was a gleam of humour in the darkness of his eyes.

'And modest as well,' Paige laughed.

'Admit it, you could have done a lot worse.'

'I could have done a lot worse,' she said huskily.

There was a tense atmosphere between them for a moment.

His eyes moved over her face. 'You were standing on these steps the first time I saw you. Do you remember?'

The sudden change of conversation threw her. 'Yes, of course I remember.' She laughed as she thought about it. 'I was a dreadfully gawky girl, wasn't I?'

'You'd a cute smile.' His eyes travelled thoughtfully over her face. 'You still do.'

Her heart flipped wildly. She wanted him so much.

He looked away from her towards the countryside. 'What were you—thirteen?'

'Yes.' She nodded. 'I saw you the first day Dad and I moved in here. I remember it very clearly. I'd met my grandfather for the first time.' Her eyes scanned the land around them. 'He and Dad had fallen out years before. I don't know what it was about—maybe Dad gambled even back then. It was only when my mother died that they made it up.' She glanced across at Brad. 'Just think if Dad and Grandad hadn't had that argument...whatever it was. I might have been born here; the first time you saw me might have been when you dangled me on your knee as a baby.'

'Well, thanks for that, Paige Monroe,' he growled in a mock-furious tone. 'I thought it was bad enough when Carolyn accused me of robbing the cradle on the night of our benefit.'

'Fifteen years isn't really such a big gap,' Paige said quickly, annoyed now that he had mentioned Carolyn. 'Not when you get to our age.'

He laughed at that. 'You make yourself sound as old as Methuselah... You're twenty-three, for heaven's sake.'

'Yes, but at thirteen I was just a kid... Now I'm a woman.'

'Yeah...you're all woman.' He looked over at her and grinned. 'I never thought, the day I saw you here for the first time, that we would end up getting married.'

'So what did you think of me?' She couldn't resist the question.

'I thought you were a lanky, gangling schoolkid.' He laughed at her expression of annoyance. 'With a nice, cute smile,' he reminded her quickly. 'But you know I did have a gorgeous girlfriend at the time.'

'I remember her...a brunette. She wore those really skimpy white shorts and used to come over to help around your vineyard. She fluttered her eyelashes at you a lot and used to call you Honey Pie.'

'Did she?' Brad pulled a face. 'I can't say I remember that.' He shook his head then looked across at her. 'You took a lot of notice.'

'I thought you were very handsome back then,' Paige admitted, then couldn't resist adding, 'And very old.'

She laughed as he threw her a dark look. 'Take that back at once.'

'No.' She giggled as he reached out for her.

'Take it back. You thought I was gorgeous and you had a major crush on me,' he insisted, laughing as she tried to wriggle away from him.

'No, I didn't.' She laughed breathlessly as he pulled her closer and pinned her wrists together with one hand.

'Take it back,' he demanded, a teasing glint in his eye. 'Or I'll make you sorry.'

She shook her head and tried to twist away from him but even though he was only holding her gently, in a playful way, he was much too strong and she couldn't move.

He bent his head and kissed her neck. It was a whisper-soft kiss and it tickled like crazy against her sensitive skin. She chuckled helplessly and writhed beneath him. 'Stop it, stop it.'

'So take it back, then.' He straightened and grinned down at her. The sunlight dappled over him as the breeze caught the boughs of the apple tree beside the steps, shading them one moment then allowing the powerful rays of the sun to get through again. She noticed the red lights in the darkness of his hair, and a few grey strands at his temple.

The atmosphere between them changed abruptly.

His eyes moved to the softness of her body. The way he was holding her emphasised the tilt of her firm breasts, the satin smoothness of her skin. Her hair was wild and dark against the white dress she wore.

She moistened her lips as his eyes touched them.

'You know, we haven't made love for a while.' He whispered the words softly against her lips as he bent to kiss her. His voice was husky now, heavy with the scent of desire.

She took a deep, shuddering breath as his kiss deepened. He released her hands and she wound them up and around his neck, trailing her fingers softly through the darkness of his hair.

She lost herself in his caresses, his warmth, her body spinning out of control.

Then he broke away from her. His eyes locked with hers, dark and questioning.

The silence between them was intense with unspoken feelings. Her heart was racing out of control.

Then his lips curved in a mocking, teasing way. 'You do still want me... Don't you?'

Before Paige could answer, Pip sprang up from behind them and started to bark.

Brad looked around and let out a sigh of annoyance as he saw his estate manager's car pulling up in front of them.

'You found her, then, I see,' Ron said, getting out of the car with a grin as he noticed how close together they were sitting.

'Yeah...I found her.' Brad brought his arms away from Paige.

'I just wanted to remind you that you'd said you'd sign the wages slip before five-thirty. The men—'

'Oh, hell.' Brad raked a hand through his hair. 'Of course, Ron. I'm sorry, I'll come back and do it now.'

He stood up and Paige straightened her dress and ran a smoothing hand over her hair self-consciously.

'Paige, do you want to come back with me in my car?' He looked down at her.

She shook her head. 'Mine is around the corner. I'll drive back in a moment.'

He nodded and then turned to walk with Ron towards his car. Pip scampered madly to get down the steps and into the car with him, as if frightened to be left behind.

As Brad drove away, she thought about his kiss. Maybe all wasn't lost after all.

She breathed in the softly scented summer air. She should have told him about the baby, but she kept putting it off, waiting for the right moment. She would tell him tonight, when they returned from the party, she decided suddenly.

Paige applied her lipstick and then stood up to step into the midnight-blue dress.

It did incredible things for her figure. She was very

slender, no sign that she was pregnant at all; if anything she was thinner now than she had been before.

She glanced at her gold wristwatch. Brad was cutting it fine. They were supposed to be at the party by seven. It was six-fifteen now and the hall was a thirty-minute ride away.

He came into the bedroom just as she was struggling to fasten her necklace.

'Sorry, honey.' He glanced at her, then came over to help her with the fastener on her necklace. 'You look fabulous,' he said softly. The touch of his fingers against her skin, the warmth of his voice caused a glow to light inside her.

'Thank you...but we have no time for all that now. You've got to hurry.'

'Have I?' He frowned, then glanced at his watch. 'Damn it all,' he said, racing to turn on the shower.

Paige had to laugh. 'I'll wait for you downstairs.'

She reached for her silk stole, which she had left on the chair at her dressing table.

She was sipping a glass of iced water when he came downstairs. He looked so handsome in the dark suit. Tall and broad-shouldered, very sophisticated. Her eyes met the darkness of his and a flare of deep yearning sprang from nowhere.

'Pity about this afternoon.' He grinned at her. 'Maybe we can pick up where we left off before too long?' His eyebrows lifted in a half-teasing, half-serious way that made her laugh. 'Let's see if we can sneak away early... Shall we?'

She smiled and felt herself melt as he pulled her closer to kiss her passionately on the lips.

She was still trembling from his touch as they made their way out to the car.

The sun was going down in a blazing ball of orange.

It lit everything with its fiery tongue, giving the world a dreamlike glow that seemed to match Paige's mood.

The party was to commemorate the fiftieth birthday of the large country club on the outskirts of town. Ticket sales for the event had been an unprecedented success, reflected in the fact that the large car park at the front of the club was practically full.

Brad found a space and together they walked up towards the blaze of light and the sound of music that spilled from the building.

'Paige, nice to see you.' Eric came immediately to her side as they stepped into the ballroom. He kissed her warmly on the cheek and Paige caught Brad's sardonically amused smile over his shoulder.

'Told you...' he mouthed. 'Big crush.'

Paige grinned and shook her head.

They were separated for a while as different people claimed their attention.

Paige missed Rosie's company. She thought about her friend, so cosy at home, deeply involved with her new baby. Mike had said there was no way they could make tonight when she had rung earlier. She hadn't really expected them to, but it had been worth a try.

Brad brought her a glass of white wine. She accepted it, but only because she didn't want to make it obvious to him that she was no longer drinking. She stood nursing it as different people came to talk and then surreptitiously she put it down on a table.

'Hope that's not alcohol you are indulging in?'

The playful voice behind her made her whirl around. 'Rosie! I thought you couldn't come.'

Rosie grinned. 'Mike's mother said she'd babysit for a couple of hours and to be honest I was crazy to get out. I've been nowhere for two whole months. We just bought tickets at the door.'

'How's William?' Brad joined them for a moment.

'A gorgeous bundle of trouble,' Rosie said wryly. 'I haven't had a decent night's sleep for ages.'

'You look well on it, anyway,' Brad said with a smile.

'I love your husband, Paige,' Rosie said, putting her arm around him.

'Oh, yes... What is this leading up to?' Brad enquired with a gleam in his eye.

'Two things...' Rosie grinned at Paige. 'He knows me so well.'

'Fire away,' Brad said easily.

'First, I've already asked Paige to be godmother to William... Will you be godfather?'

'Depends if I can find any spats and...' Brad trailed off and laughed. 'I'd be honoured, Rosie.' He grinned. 'I thought for a moment you were going to ask us to babysit.'

'You can if you want,' Rosie said quickly. 'Get some practice in—' She broke off as she saw the panic-stricken look in Paige's eyes. 'Anyway, the second thing is,' she continued swiftly, trying to cover that mistake, 'what are you doing on the afternoon of—?' She broke away from Brad and searched in her handbag as she spoke. 'Ah, here we are,' she said as she found her diary and brought it out to tell them the relevant date.

There was a moment's awkward silence. That was the date of their anniversary, a day Paige had been trying not to think about.

'I...I don't know, Rosie,' she said stiffly, hardly daring to look at Brad.

'Well, have a think and get back to me,' Rosie said with a shrug. 'Mike and I are planning a barbecue... Nothing special, just the family.'

Somebody came and claimed Brad's attention and Rosie took Paige by the arm.

'Haven't you told him about the baby yet?' she asked, her eyes wide.

'There hasn't been a good time...' Paige bit down on her lip. 'I'm going to tell him tonight.'

'Good. I'm dying to let Mike in on the news.'

Mike came over to stand next to them. 'And William cried all last night.' Rosie swiftly changed the subject.

Paige chose a glass of pure orange juice from the tray of a passing waiter.

Across the room her eyes suddenly locked on Carolyn. As always, she was dressed for maximum impact. She was wearing a long, shiny black dress. It was very tight against her body, emphasising her cleavage and the slender proportions of her waist and hips.

Rosie followed her glance. 'I suppose you know that Carolyn has split from her husband?' she remarked in a low tone.

'I had heard something.' Paige tried not to sound interested.

'I'm surprised to see her here tonight. I had heard she was down in San Francisco this weekend to get the wheels in motion for her divorce.'

'So they are definitely getting a divorce, then?' Paige felt her heart grow very cold at that information. 'How do you know that?'

Rosie shrugged. 'You know what a big village this place is... News travels pretty damn fast. There is even talk that she might be moving back to this area...despite all that rhetoric on how she didn't like it around here any longer.'

She didn't like the area, but she did want Brad, Paige thought despondently.

She turned her thoughts away from that and remembered the way Brad had kissed her this afternoon...remembered how he had wanted to make love to her. But then maybe that was because Carolyn was going away. Brad was a red-blooded male and if Carolyn wasn't available...

She frowned, utterly disgusted that she could think such a thing. Maybe Brad was seeing the other woman, but he wouldn't make love to her...he wouldn't be unfaithful until their agreement was at an end. Or was that an incredibly naive supposition?

Her adrenalin pumped wildly as she saw Brad go across to talk to Carolyn.

Then her attention was diverted by something Mike said and when she looked back Carolyn and Brad were no longer in sight.

Paige's eyes darted around the room looking for them, but it was extremely crowded.

The dance floor was packed to capacity but she couldn't see them amongst the swaying couples. Mike and Rosie were deep in conversation. Paige excused herself and walked further around the room, her eyes scanning the crowds.

She didn't feel well suddenly. Maybe it was the crowd; maybe it was the fact that she was panicking. She headed for the doors to the garden, intending to get a breath of night air.

It was warm outside, but nothing like the intensity of the heat inside.

She stood on the porch alone for a moment, taking deep breaths of air, trying to compose her foolish imagination.

The sound of a lighter being struck from the other side of the porch made her turn with a frown.

Carolyn stood alone in the shadows. She was momentarily illuminated by the flare of light as she lit a cigarette.

'Why, Paige...what a surprise. You're not out here waiting for a passionate assignation, are you?' She laughed. 'Maybe with Eric...or that other nice young chap you danced with at the benefit... What was his name?'

Paige was momentarily taken aback by the openly bitchy tone. 'Now then, Carolyn, why would I be interested in anybody else when I have Brad?' She tried to make light of the remark. 'I am very much in love with my husband.'

'How touching.' Carolyn merely smiled and walked closer. 'And there Brad and I were, hoping you would do us a favour and run away with somebody.'

'Is that your idea of a joke?' Paige was enraged by the cool nerve of that statement.

'Come on, Paige, you know very well that there is still something between Brad and me. As soon as we saw each other again the attraction was there.' Carolyn shrugged. 'I know Brad has tried to fight it, but it won't go away. Call it chemistry if you like.'

'Or fantasy.' Paige retorted swiftly. 'Why don't you do me a favour and keep your hands off my husband? You don't love him.'

'How do you know that?' She inhaled on her cigarette and then threw it down to grind it out beneath her high heels. 'Brad and I are very close...just like old times.' She regarded Paige from beneath lowered lashes.

'If you were so close, why did you finish with him and marry Robert Hicks?' Paige demanded angrily. 'If you loved him, you wouldn't have hurt him.'

For a second there was a flicker of surprise in the cool eyes. Then she smiled. 'Robert promised me the earth...swept me off my feet.' She shrugged. 'It was a mistake... I've paid for it and Brad has forgiven me.'

When Paige made no reply, she smiled. 'Brad still loves me, you know. Oh, he wouldn't want you to know that—he feels very protective of you—but then he's quite the gentleman, isn't he?'

Heat and distress licked their way through Paige's body. She forced herself not to lose her composure in front of the other woman, but it was a real struggle.

'Don't kid yourself, Carolyn,' she told her with unfaltering, cold clarity. 'Brad just feels sorry for you because you are going through a rough time at the moment. I think its despicable that you should try to take advantage of that situation.'

A shadow flickered over Carolyn's confident smile. 'You've got a nerve to talk about taking advantage,' she said, the coolness melting towards anger in her voice. 'At least I'm not a gold-digger like you.'

Paige frowned. 'What the hell do you mean by that?'

Carolyn shrugged slender shoulders. 'I know all about the money problems you had before you married Brad,' she said. 'I know that your father was a compulsive gambler and that Brad had to pull him back several times from the brink of bankruptcy.'

'How do you know that?' Paige's voice was far from steady.

'Brad and I don't have any secrets.' She smiled as she saw the sudden pallor of Paige's skin.

Paige pushed a trembling hand through her hair. She felt sick inside now…sick with grief and despair.

'He's never loved you, Paige,' Carolyn mocked. 'He was on the rebound from me and he just felt plain sorry for you.'

Carolyn looked triumphant for a moment as she saw the distress on Paige's face. Then she turned away and went back in to the party.

The sound of music and laughter from inside seemed unnaturally loud in Paige's head as the door opened and closed behind the other woman.

'He's never loved you…' Carolyn's words raced around and around in her head.

She let out her breath in a trembling sigh. Slowly she followed Carolyn back inside.

Brad was up on the stage at the far end of the room.

He was talking about the evening, and the special role the club had played in the community over the years.

The fact that he had discussed her situation with Carolyn was incredibly hurtful. But then she was the woman he really loved, the woman he had wanted to marry.

There was thunderous applause as Brad finished his speech and started to come down from the stage. He looked over at Paige and smiled.

She couldn't smile back. The room felt as if it was spinning. She felt dizzy, very hot.

She put a hand on the nearest table.

'Are you all right, Paige?' someone asked.

She was aware that there was a murmur of concern around her, but she couldn't focus properly.

The next moment she felt Brad's arms around her. Then she blacked out completely.

# CHAPTER ELEVEN

WHEN Paige opened her eyes she was being cradled in Brad's arms as he carried her outside.

Paige could hear Rosie's voice, gentle and reassuring. 'She'll be OK after some fresh air.'

'God, I hope so.' Brad's voice was deep with concern and Paige tried desperately to come around properly, shake off the fuzzy haze that seemed to be clouding her mind.

'She hasn't been well for a while now; I should have insisted she went to see a doctor.' He put her gently down on one of the chairs outside. 'Paige...Paige, can you hear me?' One arm was still holding her as he crouched down beside her.

'I think Dr Riley is here; they are looking for him inside.' Rosie moved forward. She held a glass of water. 'Paige, do you think a drink would help?' she asked calmly.

'I don't want the doctor,' Paige murmured. 'I'm OK now.'

She was starting to come around. Perhaps it was the fear that her doctor was here, that he would come and tell Brad that he had seen her only a few weeks ago and that she was pregnant.

'You'll have to see the doctor.' Brad took the glass from Rosie and held it against Paige's lips while she took a few sips.

The cool liquid made her feel better. 'It was just the heat...' she said unsteadily. 'There's no need to make a fuss.'

'I think we've already done that,' Rosie said wryly.

She met her friend's eyes. 'Are you really OK?' she asked her softly.

Paige nodded. 'I just need to go home and lie down, then I'll be fine.'

'She is starting to get some colour back in her cheeks,' Rosie remarked to Brad. 'Maybe it would be best if you just took her home. You can always call Dr Riley out tomorrow morning.'

Brad frowned. 'I don't know. I'd rather he saw her now.' He stood up. 'Look after her for a minute, Rosie; I'll just see if they've managed to locate him.'

Rosie knelt down beside her, then cast a glance over her shoulder to where a few other people were standing anxiously watching. 'She'll be all right now,' Rosie said cheerfully. 'Perhaps you'd just give us some space?'

Immediately they started to filter back into the hall.

'Have I made a dreadful spectacle of myself?' Paige asked remorsefully.

'No, only a few hundred or so witnessed Brad carrying you out.' Rosie grinned as Paige looked at her in alarm. 'It wasn't as bad as that.'

'Any minute now Dr Riley will be out and then it really will be that bad,' Paige said with a groan. 'I don't want Brad to find out like this.'

'I think Dr Riley must have gone home, otherwise he would have been straight out here,' Rosie said reassuringly. 'Are you sure you feel OK? Everything all right with the baby?'

Paige nodded.

'Then go home with Brad and talk to him,' Rosie said earnestly. 'Tell him, Paige. Don't put it off any longer.'

Brad came back out to join them. 'Riley left some time ago, apparently.'

'Well, Paige is feeling a lot better now. Just take her home.'

Paige started to get up from her chair and Brad came immediately to put an arm around her.

Paige smiled at Rosie. 'I'll ring you in the morning. Thanks, Rosie.'

The powerful headlights on Brad's car sliced through the darkness of the long, straight road ahead as they made their way home.

'How are you feeling now?' Brad asked anxiously.

'Don't fuss, Brad...please. I'm fine.'

There was a heavy silence between them until he drove the car through the gates to the vineyard and the house came into sight.

'Have you seen much of Carolyn since she came back?' Her voice was remarkably calm considering the wealth of emotion inside her.

'I've seen her on a few occasions. She came into the office one day and we had a drink—'

'Tea and sympathy?' Paige grated wryly, the fact that he wasn't trying to cover up that he'd seen the other woman rubbing raw over a blaze of jealousy.

He brought the car to a standstill and switched off the engine. They were parked under the shadow of the huge eucalyptus trees; Paige could smell their fresh, tangy scent in the night air.

He turned and looked at her. 'You could call it that. She wanted to tell me about her marriage break-up.'

'How cosy. You swapped stories, I take it. She told you about her divorce and you told her about our arrangement.'

'I've never mentioned our arrangement.'

'Liar.' Her voice broke angrily. 'She knows all my personal history. She knows about my father's gambling and my money problems before I met you.'

'Paige, I have never spoken a word to Carolyn about any of that.'

'So how did she know?'

He sighed. 'She was at my house the night your father came over to ask for an extension on his loan. I asked her to wait outside while we talked.' He shrugged. 'But your father lost his temper and…well, there were raised voices. She overheard everything.'

She should have been relieved that he hadn't told her, but all Paige could think was how close he was to Carolyn. They had no secrets. She realised she had been kidding herself all this time. Brad still loved Carolyn and the two of them were just waiting for the time when they were together again.

Her heart hammered like crazy as she reached for the door handle and got out of the car, her legs feeling decidedly shaky as she walked up to the house.

Brad was close behind her as she stepped in through the front door. The hallway was lit by the softness of side lamps, which threw warm pink light over the parquet floor, the rich tapestry rugs.

'Look, Paige. I wouldn't worry about Carolyn saying anything about your father to anyone else. I did ask her not to repeat what she had overheard. I suppose she thought it didn't matter if she repeated it to you.'

'Well, it does matter.' Paige hated the way he defended the other woman.

'It's all in the past, Paige,' Brad said gently.

'It's not, though, is it, Brad? It's with us now. It's the reason we are together at all.' She swung around to look at him and felt suddenly weak, as if all this was too much and her body was crying out for her just to stop.

'Paige?' He came across to her quickly, and put a hand on her arm. 'Come on, let's get you upstairs. You are really not well enough to stand here having a discussion.'

She didn't argue, but allowed him to help her up the stairs.

It was a relief to sit down on the bed.

She watched as Brad bent to help her take off her shoes. 'I'm going to ring Dr Riley first thing in the morning,' he said.

She reached out a hand and touched the darkness of his hair tenderly, remembering suddenly the night he had proposed to her. Her dreams that one day he would grow to love her had been absurd. She realised that now very clearly.

'If you don't feel well enough to go to the surgery, then the doctor can come here,' Brad continued briskly. 'You should have gone to see him ages ago when you first felt ill.'

'I did.'

He frowned and looked up at her. 'You did?'

She nodded, then took a deep breath. Now was as good a time as any to tell him the truth. She had no illusions left about their future together. 'I'm pregnant, Brad...'

For a second the look of shock on his face was almost amusing.

'Pregnant?' He stared at her incredulously.

She nodded.

'Why didn't you tell me? How far along are you?' He sounded stunned.

'About ten weeks. Look, it's a mistake, but it's my mistake and I'll deal with it,' she told him, trying to be brisk...trying to sound controlled and confident.

'What do you mean you'll deal with it?' His voice darkened ominously.

'I mean it's my baby and I'm taking full responsibility—'

She broke off as he gave a laugh of complete and utter amazement. 'You'll do no such thing.' He raked a hand through his hair. 'Maybe you missed a couple of lessons at school, Paige, but I can assure you that it takes two to make a baby. This is my responsibility as much as yours.'

'Don't be facetious. I'm trying to tell you that this doesn't mean we have to be tied to each other.'

He shook his head. Then he stood up and walked away from her towards the window as if he was trying to gather his thoughts in private. He stood with his back to her for a moment in silence. 'How long have you known?'

She didn't answer him immediately and he turned to glare at her.

'I don't know.' She shrugged helplessly. 'I...I suppose I knew for sure the morning we went to see Rosie in hospital.'

'That's weeks ago.' He shook his head again. 'I'm stunned by your arrogant assumption that you are the only one able to make a decision on what we should do.' He sounded very angry now. His eyes were incredibly hard and dark and they seemed to slice into her. 'I take it you are planning on just moving out of my life anyway?'

'I don't think a baby is a good enough reason for us to stay together.' She spoke quietly.

His eyes narrowed now. 'So what were you planning to do? Take my baby and waltz off to Seattle to see your old boyfriend? I hate to burst whatever romantic bubbles are going around in your head, Paige, but that is my child and you are going nowhere.'

'You can't tell me where I can go and what I can do.' She shook her head. 'We have a business agreement, Brad. What was it you said right back at the beginning? Children aren't part of this arrangement—I'm not planning on starting a family with you?' Her eyes shimmered. 'Forgive me if I'm not word-perfect, but I think that was how the conversation went.'

'I was trying to be responsible,' he retorted furiously. 'Children are a lifelong commitment—'

'And you didn't want a lifelong commitment with me.' She cut across him swiftly. 'I know, I signed the damn contract. I agreed to the terms. I don't want to be stuck in a loveless marriage for life either.'

For a second he looked as if she had struck him. She glanced away, her voice raw. 'I'm sorry if that hurts your male ego, but you know it's true. And I can assure you that I have no romantic bubbles floating around in my head; they were burst a long time ago.' She closed her eyes over the mental picture of Brad taking Carolyn into his arms.

'Do you even want the baby?' He grated the words unevenly.

Her eyes flew open to meet his. 'Yes, of course I want it.' Her voice was firmly decisive. 'So if you are going to suggest that I...I get rid of it or have it adopted or something, then you're wasting your time.' Her voice broke slightly under the weight of emotional feeling.

'I wasn't going to suggest that for a minute.' He took a deep breath and came over to crouch back down beside her, staring earnestly up into her face. 'I'd have thought you'd know me a bit better than that by now.' He took hold of her hands. 'Is that why you didn't tell me you were pregnant...because you thought I'd try and talk you into getting rid of the baby?'

'No.' She looked into his eyes, the sorrow in his expression tearing her apart. 'No...it wasn't that. I do know you better than that.' Her lips twisted wryly. 'I suppose I thought you'd tell me that we should stay together for the sake of the baby...and I was afraid.'

'Afraid to stay?' His voice was very low and husky.

'Afraid because it wasn't what we planned,' she admitted honestly. 'I don't want us to end up hating each other, Brad, feeling resentful, trapped.'

'I don't want that either,' he said heavily.

'So it's best that we split up—'

'No.' He cut across her forcefully. 'I can't let you go, Paige.' His eyes moved over the shimmering light in her eyes, the soft, vulnerable curve of her lips. 'Not now.'

She looked away from him and didn't know whether to cry out of sheer relief or sheer despair, because she knew that deep down he wanted Carolyn. But Brad's sense of duty was too strong to allow him just to follow his heart and be damned with the consequences... No matter what the personal cost to himself he would stand by her. In truth she had known that this would be his reaction. If she had any pride at all she should turn him down.

'It might not be what we planned, Paige, but fate works in strange ways. Maybe somebody is telling us that it damn well should have been what we planned?' He looked at her, a teasing, warm light in his eyes now as he lifted her chin up and forced her to look directly at him once more.

'Don't you think we owe it to our baby to give our marriage a try?' he asked softly when she made no reply. 'I think we could make it work.'

'Even without love?'

He looked at her bleakly for a moment. 'Is there any greater love than a parent's love for a child? Wouldn't we be bonded through that?'

She looked away from him. Could he sacrifice his love for Carolyn without regret...and should she accept him on those terms? she wondered. She had to think what would be best for their child.

'I don't think I'd make a bad dad,' Brad said, a smile curving his lips. 'I'd be firm but fun. I'd read bedtime stories and do bathtime duties... Hell, I'll even do nappy-changing if you want. I'll borrow that book from Mike and swot up on everything.'

Paige had to laugh as she wiped the mist of tears from her eyes. 'Don't you dare borrow that book; it's driven Rosie mad.'

He smiled at her. 'What do you say? Will you give me a chance to try my hand as a modern-day dad?'

She swallowed hard and felt such love for him that it almost overwhelmed her. She would have given Brad Monroe anything.

She put her arms around him and went into the circle of his arms, burying her head against his shoulder, her pride crumbling into a million pieces. 'Just take me to bed, Brad, and hold me,' she whispered softly.

# CHAPTER TWELVE

'DO YOU think he'll like it?' Paige held up the gold watch to show Rosie.

'There is something wrong with him if he doesn't,' Rosie said with a laugh. 'It's a lovely present, Paige.'

It was late afternoon and they were driving back from town in Rosie's car after a fraught session of shopping. Fraught because William had been fractious in every shop they had gone into, crying loudly despite all attempts to placate him with milk, with toys, with cuddles... Nothing had worked until they were outside and then mysteriously he'd been all smiles again.

Paige cast a glance around at the child now. He was in his car seat in the back and he was fast asleep, his long dark lashes sooty-soft against his creamy baby skin.

'Poor little mite must have been tired,' Paige murmured with a smile as she returned her attention to her friend.

Rosie shook her head and grinned. 'He would be. I tell you, Wills is a typical man; they are born like that. Mike is exactly the same when I drag him into a shop: whines and moans until he can get out.'

Paige laughed and started to put the watch she had bought for Brad back into the box.

'What do you think Brad will buy you?' Rosie asked.

Paige shrugged. 'I don't know.'

'Heck, it's only a couple of days to your anniversary. I'd have put in my order by now.'

In fact, her anniversary was tomorrow, but Paige didn't correct her friend; she didn't want any fuss.

'We haven't talked about it, Rosie,' she admitted now.

Actually there was slight unease about the subject. Paige knew she would just feel relief when the date had passed. She didn't know how Brad would feel.

He had been wonderful to her these last few weeks, had treated her with gentleness and understanding. But since the night she had told him she was pregnant they hadn't talked much about the future, had trodden warily around the subject as if it was taboo. And they hadn't made love. At first Paige hadn't worried about that. She hadn't been feeling well and she'd supposed the time wasn't right. But as the weeks had gone by and she'd started to feel stronger Brad still hadn't shown any real interest in her. They lay together in the large double bed, but emotionally Paige felt he was somewhere else; she tried not to think where.

'I'd send out a few hints if I were you,' Rosie said, cutting into her thoughts.

'On what?' Paige was momentarily lost.

'Your anniversary present,' Rosie said, a glint of mischief in her eyes. 'You know the kind of thing. I saw a lovely diamond yesterday, and solitaires are really big fashion this year, darling, and I mean big.'

'It's no wonder Mike nearly passes out when you take him into a shop,' Paige laughed.

'Talking about passing out, how did your last check-up go?' Rosie asked humorously.

'Fine. Dr Riley was most reassuring. He told Brad to stop worrying.' Paige grinned.

'He was worried about you that night you passed out,' Rosie said with a shake of her head. 'But then you did look dreadful. I've never seen anyone go so white... Except maybe Mike when he gets the credit card bill.'

Rosie pulled her car to a standstill in front of Paige's home. 'Whose is the green sports car?'

'I've no idea,' Paige said. 'Someone to see Brad. He's doing some paperwork from home for the next few days.' She unfastened her seat belt. 'Will you come in for a coffee?'

Rosie glanced over at the sleeping baby in the back. 'Better not. I'll get junior home. He'll be ready for a feed soon.'

'OK. Thanks for braving the shops with me.' Paige started to gather up her bags.

'I'm just sorry we had to cut the trip short,' Rosie said with a smile. 'But then I don't think either of us could have taken another bout of crying. Now, don't forget we are having a barbecue tomorrow afternoon. Nothing fancy, just family. Come about twelve-thirty.'

Paige hesitated. In the lead-up to her anniversary she had forgotten that Rosie was having a barbecue on the same day.

'You can still come?' Rosie asked, her eyes widening.

'Oh, yes. It's kind of you,' Paige said quickly. She was sure Brad hadn't organised anything for tomorrow. Maybe they would both find it easier to be with friends and not have to think about the date.

'OK, twelve-thirty,' Rosie said again as Paige reached to kiss her cheek. 'See you then.'

As soon as Paige pushed open the front door she recognised Carolyn's voice.

She put her carrier bags down on the hall table just as Carolyn and Brad walked through from the lounge.

The woman was dressed very elegantly in a tailored blue trouser suit, her long, blonde hair as always perfectly styled in smooth, sleek waves.

'Paige, what a nice surprise. I'm glad I caught you before I left,' she said immediately. Her manner was so sickly sweet and false that Paige knew a wild, irrational moment when she just wanted to open the door and sling her out.

Instead, she forced herself to face up to the situation and not give in to the anger and apprehension she felt at the other woman's presence in her home. 'And what brings you out here, Carolyn?' she asked.

'I've just come to say goodbye. I'm going back to San Francisco tomorrow. Robert and I have come to an amicable decision on our waterfront property, but there is still a lot to sort out.'

Paige noticed suddenly that the woman's eyes were slightly swollen, as if she had been crying a lot. She felt a sudden and unexpected pang of sympathy for her.

'Brad's been telling me about the baby. I believe congratulations are in order.'

'Yes.' Paige's voice was very strained. She wondered if Brad had told her the baby was a mistake but that he felt honour-bound to stay with her now. She forced herself to say very brightly, 'We are…both…pleased about it.' Her eyes shimmered, over-bright with emotion as she looked at Brad.

For a moment, the usual good humour in the darkness of his eyes was replaced by an expression of such melancholy that it made her heart slam against her ribs.

'I bet you are.' There was a slight edge to the other woman's voice now, an edge of derision and bitterness. Then she glanced at her wristwatch. 'Well, I'd better go. I've got a long drive ahead of me.' She reached to kiss Brad on the cheek. 'Take care,' she breathed softly as she moved a step back from him.

'You too,' Brad said gently.

The shrill ring of the telephone cut through the tense silence that descended suddenly.

'I'll get that.' Brad moved away. He lifted his hand in a salute to Carolyn, but he didn't look back at her as he disappeared into his study.

There was a moment of silence as Paige desperately tried to come to terms with the fact that Brad was so upset about this parting.

Carolyn walked towards the front door.

'Are you driving down to San Francisco now?' Paige followed her slowly.

'Yes...I am. I'm sure that comes as a big relief to you,' Carolyn answered bluntly.

Paige didn't answer. Yes, she felt relief...relief tinged with guilt that she was standing in the way of Brad's happiness. He obviously wanted Carolyn with all his heart. She had never seen him look so heartsore as he had in that second. It was as if the mask of confidence and bravado had slipped for just a few precious moments, allowing a glimpse of his true feelings.

If she were a better person she would go into Brad's study now and tell him to take Carolyn, to follow his heart and be damned with the consequences, she told herself fiercely. Her hands clenched into tight fists at the thought. Maybe it was weak and selfish of her, but she didn't honestly think she had the strength to do that. She needed Brad so much...not because she was having his baby, but because she loved him so, so much.

She couldn't give him up, at least not without some kind of effort for a little while longer to see if their relationship would work.

'I hope all goes well for you,' she said softly now to Carolyn and surprisingly she did mean it.

'That's very benevolent of you.' Carolyn's eyes swept over Paige's appearance in the long white skirt and cotton top. Her pregnancy wasn't really showing very much, particularly under her loose clothing. 'But then I suppose you can afford to be benevolent. You've managed to use the oldest trick in the book to hold onto your man... I just hope you can live with the knowledge that it's me he really loves.'

'That isn't true, Carolyn,' Paige said in a low trembling tone.

'No? We'll see.' Carolyn smiled. 'You may have won the battle, but the war most certainly isn't over. I've given Brad my telephone number in San Francisco and my address. He'll come back to me one day, maybe not this year and maybe not the next, but given time he'll realise that life is too precious to squander in a loveless marriage.'

'I think you should go now, Carolyn.' Paige was very cool and calm. 'Before you make an even bigger fool of yourself.'

The woman looked taken aback by the comment. She frowned, then, with a shake of her head, she walked out of the front door.

For a long moment Paige just stood in the hall, her emotions raw. Then she moved towards Brad's study.

He was still on the phone, listening intently to who-ever was on the other end of the line.

Paige leaned in the doorway and watched him.

He smiled up at her for just a brief second before reaching for his diary. 'Can we schedule it for one day next week? No…no, that's no good.'

His voice flowed over her senses, deep and confident. He had obviously got his emotions under control now, had cocooned himself in business. That was what people did when they were unhappy in a marriage, wasn't it? Turned themselves in, focused themselves on something else, something all-consuming to hide behind.

Her eyes drank in the lean, handsome features.

'He'll come back to me one day, maybe not this year and maybe not the next, but given time he'll realise that life is too precious to squander in a loveless marriage.' Carolyn's words played through her head.

Brad put the phone down with a sigh and looked over at her. 'She's gone, I take it?' For a brief second there was a harsh edge to the words.

She nodded.

He leaned back in his chair and looked at her.

'How long was she here?'

'I don't know. Mrs O'Brien made us coffee before she left for the afternoon.' He shrugged. 'I suppose about an hour or so.' He busied himself writing something in his diary and then shutting it away in the drawer again.

'She looked as if she had been crying.' Paige couldn't leave the subject, although she wished to heaven that she could.

'Yeah…well.' Brad shrugged and raked an impatient hand through his hair as if he didn't really want to think about that. 'She is upset. She'll be OK, though.' He looked at her firmly. 'She'll meet somebody else. Life goes on, doesn't it?'

'Not always as we'd want it to, though,' Paige said softly, her eyes shadowed.

'No…not always as we'd want it.' There was a brief moment of huskiness in his tone.

She turned away and went to pick up her shopping from the hall table. Brad followed her out.

'What have you been buying?' His voice was deliberately light-hearted and she knew that he was making a determined effort to get the atmosphere between them back to normal.

'I got some decorating books and some baby books that Rosie thought I should have.' It took a lot of strength and determination to meet him halfway.

'Oh, good, a little night-time reading for me to be getting on with.' Brad's lips twisted in a teasing, warm smile and then he looked down at her in a way that just melted her heart.

'I…I thought we'd decorate that small bedroom next to ours for the baby; what do you think?'

'Let's have a look.' Brad took her hand and together they went upstairs. The touch of his hand against hers stirred up such a yearning inside, a feeling that didn't go away even when he let go of her to push open the door into the small box room.

The room was bright and airy, with the same views over the vineyard that their bedroom had.

'I thought we could paint it yellow; that way it doesn't matter whether we have a boy or a girl.' Paige tried to sound practical, tried to sound as if, hidden behind the words, her heart wasn't about to break.

Brad looked thoughtful for a moment.

She supposed that, like her, he was making a determined effort to be positive, to look to the future and try to forget what might have been with Carolyn.

'We could knock a door directly through to our room from here.' He pointed to the side of the wardrobe. 'Then we could leave the door open and always be sure of hearing him cry.'

'If he's anything like William I think we'll hear him crying from six rooms away.' Paige smiled gently. 'And anyway, who's to say it will be a him? I wouldn't mind a little girl.'

Brad smiled back at her, then put an arm around her shoulder. 'It doesn't matter what we have, does it? As long as it's healthy and happy.'

For a moment she leaned against him, her body drinking in the deep reassurance of his arms.

'I suppose I should get back to work,' Brad said with a sigh as he pulled away from her. 'This is the only drawback about working from home; there are far too many distractions.'

He glanced at his watch. 'Mrs O'Brien finished early today; she's gone to visit her sister or something. What do you say we go out to dinner?'

'I was going to cook us something.' Paige hoped her skin didn't look hot and red. She had asked Mrs O'Brien to take the afternoon off. She had wanted the opportunity to cook for Brad. Had planned a romantic meal, candle-light, soft music and all the trimmings, in the hope, she supposed, of kindling the passion that had been missing from their relationship throughout the last weeks.

Now, in the light of Carolyn's visit, she wondered if such an idea wasn't whimsical in the extreme. It was one thing talking and planning for their future with the purpose and motivation of their baby in mind; it was quite another to put the emphasis of that child aside for an evening and concentrate solely on each other.

Brad looked amused for a moment. 'Are you sure you want to cook? I've still a lot to do this afternoon, so I won't be finished until late.'

Paige thought about it for a moment then shrugged. If she didn't try, if she didn't make some effort, then she might as well just have told Carolyn that she had won Brad's heart anyway. 'Tell me what time you'd like to eat and I'll organise everything for then.'

'All right, if that's what you want.' Brad kissed the side of her cheek lightly. 'I'll see you later.'

After he had gone, Paige picked up her bags and brought them through to the bedroom. She had one last look at the watch she had bought for Brad, then put it away in the top drawer of her dressing table, before going downstairs.

She went through to the lounge. The cups and saucers were still on the coffee table from Carolyn's visit. Paige noticed from the cups and the way the cushions were arranged that they had been sitting quite close to each other on the settee. There was a tissue box next to the coffee pot.

Paige stacked the dishes back on the tray and then plumped up the cushions with brisk, quick movements. She didn't want to think about the scene in here. She didn't want to dwell on the emotional turmoil that must have erupted when Brad had told Carolyn that he was staying with her, his wife, out of duty. She closed her mind to it, just as she had been trying to close her mind to the thought of Brad with Carolyn since she had seen them in each other's arms.

'It was a lovely meal, Paige. Thank you,' Brad said, looking across at her.

They were seated at the table in the dining room. The soft gleam of candlelight reflected on the crystal glasses and the silverware on the table. The French windows beside them were open slightly, with a view out towards the darkness of the garden. A full moon hung low in the sky, its silver light glittering over the swimming pool like a light sprinkling of diamonds.

Paige smiled. 'Well, it's not often that Mrs O'Brien allows me into her kitchen. It's almost like a sacred domain with her.'

'Maybe we should chase her out more often. This reminds me of the dinner we had that night at your house before we got married.'

'The night we decided we should have a marriage contract,' she reflected.

'I thought it was a good idea,' he said with a shrug. 'It allowed us to forget the business side of things and trust each other a little more...'

'Maybe what we need now is a more up-to-date, pre-baby contract, so that we can be even more businesslike and practical.' The words slipped out, jesting yet hard-edged, underlining the fact that despite her outward appearance of being calm and relaxed she was anything but. 'I'm sorry, Brad.' She cut across him as he made to speak. 'That wasn't funny.'

Silence descended between them.

'I know you are not happy about this situation, Paige.' He raked a hand through his hair. 'I'm not wildly ecstatic about it either. I never envisaged us having to stay together because of a child. But I'm going to do my best to make sure this works, that—'

'Maybe you shouldn't bother.' Paige scraped her chair back from the table, her temper and her emotions just snapping. 'In fact, I'd rather you didn't. I'd rather you weren't so damn noble and righteous. I managed fine on my own once before...I'll manage again. I don't need you.'

She turned away from him and stood at the open French windows, breathing in the night air and trying to think calmly. She didn't want to be second best...second choice. She had her pride.

'I thought we had agreed to try?' His voice was low and calm as he got up and came to stand behind her.

'But we've got to think long term.' She squeezed her eyes tightly closed, willing herself to be strong. 'I'm thinking about your happiness as well as my own, Brad, and I just don't think we can continue with this charade. What is it they say? The road to hell is paved with good intentions? I don't doubt for one moment that your intentions are good...but this just isn't going to work.'

'It will if we're determined enough,' he said quietly. He turned her firmly so that he could look down at her.

Her eyes moved over the lean lines of his body. He was wearing a light suit that sat easily on his broad-shouldered frame. He looked so attractive that she just wanted to slip into the comfort of his arms and ask him to make love to her, ask him to make the pain go away. But she knew it wasn't going to go away... She supposed she had known it the moment she'd seen the anguish in Brad's eyes this afternoon.

'Look, Paige, I know I've made mistakes in the past. I rushed you into this marriage. I was trying to be so damn practical about how our union could be beneficial for us both, but deep down I really believed that love would grow between us. I still haven't given up on us—'

'Yes, you have. You're just trying to do what you

think is the right thing.' She bit down on her lip. 'Look, I'd be all right on my own, Brad—'

'Yeah, I know you would be. You're a strong intelligent woman and you probably wouldn't be on your own too long either.'

'Is that what's bothering you? The thought that some other man might bring up your child?'

'Yes…that bothers me. I want this child, Paige. I don't look on him or her as just a mistake, I look on it as a second chance…hope.'

There was such sincerity in his voice that Paige's eyes misted with tears of sudden emotion.

'It's our anniversary tomorrow, a whole year. Can you really say that it's been a bad year?' he asked her huskily.

She shook her head. 'No…in a lot of ways it's been wonderful.'

He smiled and touched her face tenderly. 'I know you are a big romantic…and this isn't how you pictured things. Maybe you're still in love with that old boyfriend of yours.' His lips twisted wryly. 'There's something about a first love that lingers and won't go away. But together I think we can work things out. Give me a chance, Paige, because it's what I want with all my heart.'

She stared up at him. She had tried to be so strong, to stand back and give him his freedom, but he had chosen their child over that, over his love for Carolyn.

'I don't know what to do.' Her voice quivered with emotion.

'We could go to bed and lose ourselves in making love?' He whispered the words softly against her hair.

She could smell the faint tang of whisky on his breath; it was pleasant, not too obtrusive. Brad didn't usually drink very much but had indulged in a few whiskys this evening. She wondered if, despite all the strong talk, he was as unsure about this as she was.

She looked up at him and immediately took back that last thought. There was nothing unsure about Brad.

She shut her eyes and tried to think coherently. When she had planned this evening she had wanted this to happen. Now she was torn between her need for him and the knowledge that he was probably trying to drown out the emotions inside himself, deliberately trying to shut away his feelings for Carolyn and transfer them to her.

He lowered his head. He kissed her lips, then her cheek, then he lifted the heavy length of her hair to kiss the sides of her neck.

She felt herself sway against him, desire curling instantly to life, cutting through the fragile reins of her restraint and good intentions.

# CHAPTER THIRTEEN

PAIGE was alone in the double bed when she woke up the next morning.

Sunlight dappled through the window, making leafy shadows from the trees swirl over the plain carpets and the bedspread.

She stretched out a hand towards the other side of the bed, her mind still in the deep comfort between memories of last night and the heaviness of sleep.

Making love with Brad had always been special, but last night it had seemed to Paige to be even more momentous. There had been such a deep tenderness, a gentleness in his touch. She had revelled in the caress of his hands against the soft curves of her body, absorbed the warmth of his skin next to hers, the feeling of belonging and loving.

The exquisite ecstasy lingered now in the sleepiness of her body. When they had made love all insecurities were gone, the world shut out in the greater glory of love.

'You will stay with me, won't you?' Brad had asked as the clock downstairs had chimed midnight, heralding their first anniversary. And she had whispered yes over and over again as he'd taken her to the heights of pleasure.

She sighed and sat up. 'Brad...?' Her eyes moved around the room and towards the door to the bathroom. There was no answer.

Paige got up and put on her dressing gown. She cast a quick glance in the mirror, and ran a smoothing hand over the wild silkiness of her long hair before going downstairs.

She heard Brad's voice coming from his study and she went across. Her hand was on the door when she heard him say, 'No, you did a good job; I think she believed you. I don't think she has any real idea about our plans.'

Paige frowned and hesitated.

'I'm tied by duty here for a while longer.' Brad's voice was heavy with regret for a moment. 'It's just the way the cookie crumbles and I have to accept it. But that doesn't mean I'm not going to make the most of the opportunity to get away next week. How does ten days in the Bahamas sound?' He laughed warmly. 'I thought you'd say that. No, I'm going to tell her it's a business trip upstate.'

Paige didn't know why she was so totally shocked; it wasn't as if she didn't know that Brad didn't love her. But she had never thought that he would so calmly plot to deceive her. She had believed all his talk about trying to make their marriage work…had believed that he had said goodbye to Carolyn.

She bit down on her lip. How naive could she get? Now it sounded like the whole thing yesterday with Carolyn had been contrived just to put her off the scent…that Brad was going to continue to see Carolyn…was going to take the woman to the Bahamas for ten days for heaven's sake and tell *her* it was a business trip.

She backed away from the door and retreated upstairs.

How could she have been such a blind fool? she berated herself fiercely. She paced backwards and forwards across the bedroom, her mind racing in circles. She didn't know what to do, what to say to Brad. All she knew was that she couldn't put up with this situation. She had more pride than that.

She heard Brad's footsteps in the corridor and quickly dashed towards the bathroom and turned on the shower. She couldn't face him yet, she had to pull herself together first. She might have lost her heart to Brad Monroe, but she wasn't about to lose her dignity along with it.

'Paige, I have to go out for a while,' Brad called to her through the door. 'I'll be back in time to pick you up for Rosie's barbecue. See you later.'

'See you later.' Somehow she managed to answer him…but her voice felt stiff and unnatural.

She stepped under the heavy jet of the shower and stood there for long moments just trying to come to terms with the situation.

Hell, Carolyn Hicks had been the perfect actress yesterday. Paige had honestly swallowed the tearful eyes, the look of distress. Come to that, her husband had been pretty convincing as well.

Anger blazed through her, quickly followed by an unbearable sadness.

There was no way she would be able to continue with her marriage…not now. Even for the sake of her child she couldn't possibly contemplate living such a lie.

Her mind ran ahead, picturing what it would be like. Weekends on her own knowing that Brad was with Carolyn, the lies and deceit, not being able to trust him when he said he had a business trip or a conference; it would be insufferable.

She snapped off the water briskly. She would have to ask Brad for a divorce… She had no alternative. What was it Carolyn had said yesterday? Life was too damn short to waste it in a loveless marriage. And, while she had been prepared to work at their relationship when she had thought there had just been the two of them, there was no way she would live as a part of some triangle.

*    *    *

Paige was dressed and ready to leave and still there was no sign of Brad. She glanced at her watch. It was almost twelve-fifteen. They were going to be late for Rosie at this rate. She supposed it didn't matter too much; the barbecue wouldn't be under way for a while.

She walked to the mirror and glanced at her reflection. She was carrying the baby very neatly; she still looked quite trim, the blue sheath dress showing just a hint of her pregnancy. She put a hand diffidently on her stomach. 'It looks like it's going to be just you and me, junior,' she said softly.

It wouldn't be too bad, she told herself calmly. It wasn't as if she didn't have a home to go to. Her eyes shadowed. This was where she felt her home was now...here with Brad.

The sound of the front door slamming made her turn and go out towards the landing.

'Sorry, sweetheart.' Brad raced up the stairs. He was holding a large bouquet of red roses.

'Where have you been?' Her voice wasn't entirely steady.

'Stopped off in town to get you these.' He handed her the flowers. 'I remember how you told me once that you liked to get flowers.'

'Did I?' Paige tried to act coolly.

'I remember it well.' He put a hand under her chin and tipped her face up towards his. 'Happy anniversary, darling.'

She allowed him to kiss her, her heart racing painfully against her chest, her anger fading fast as the warmth of his lips touched through to her very soul.

She pulled away from him, unable to bear the sweet torture of knowing that this was all a sham.

'I'll put these in water,' she murmured huskily. 'Hurry up, Brad, we don't want to be late.'

She had composed herself by the time Brad followed

her downstairs. She tried not to notice how handsome he looked in the smart but casual beige trousers and cream shirt. She was thankful now that they were in a rush, that there was little time to talk.

She was glad that they were just going to Rosie's and that it would be a quiet afternoon… There would be time for her to reflect on what she should say to Brad.

'You OK?' Brad flicked a glance at her as they pulled up outside Rosie and Mike's house. 'Only you've been very quiet.'

She nodded and reached to open the car door.

Rosie's house was just on the outskirts of the town, but it was still very countrified. It was a small, clapperboard residence with a quaint character. There was an orchard at the back of the house and a paddock running along the side. The field belonged to the next-door neighbour who ran a riding school and consequently there were usually a few horses going through their paces. But today the place was deserted. In fact, there was a strangely silent feel to the house. There were no cars in the drive. No sign of life at all.

'I wonder if Rosie's mum and dad couldn't make it? Their car isn't here,' Paige remarked as Brad locked the car and walked with her towards the front door.

'Maybe they're just not here yet. You see, we're not as late as you had feared.' Brad pressed the doorbell.

They stood for a while but nobody came to answer it.

'Must be out in the back garden.' Brad pushed the door and it swung open.

'Hello… Anybody home?' He shouted out as he led the way through the hall.

He caught hold of Paige's hand as they reached the kitchen. It was just a casual gesture, but it struck a raw note inside Paige. She was about to pull away from him when they stepped through the sliding glass doors into the garden. Then she forgot everything in her surprise as a huge crowd of people shouted out, 'Surprise!' in loud, cheerful voices.

A shower of rose petals fell softly over them as they stood there in bewilderment. There was a big banner saying 'Happy Anniversary, Paige and Brad' strung between the trees at the bottom of the long garden.

'Happy anniversary.' Rosie was the first to embrace them both warmly.

'You absolute horror,' Paige breathed in astonishment.

'Well, you didn't really think I had forgotten the date of your anniversary, did you?' Her friend grinned. 'This is my revenge for you two sneaking off to Las Vegas last year and doing me out of a wedding party.'

'Congratulations.' Mike stepped forward with William in his arms and kissed Paige's cheek.

Paige looked around at the sea of familiar, dear faces. Friends that both she and Brad had known all their lives. 'This is so kind of you,' she said unsteadily, for a moment completely overcome.

Champagne corks popped and a glass was pressed into Brad's hand.

'Sorry, you have to have orange juice,' Rosie said with a grin as she passed Paige her drink.

'How on earth have you had time to organise this with a new baby to see to?' Paige asked, still completely dazed.

'No problem,' Mike said easily. 'We all just wanted to wish you well for the future and tell you we are real glad that you both finally saw some sense and got married because we all think you are perfect for each other.' He raised his glass.

'Speech,' someone called from the back, and several others took up the chant.

Paige couldn't say anything, her heart was so filled with emotion. She couldn't believe that all these lovely people had come to wish them happiness for the future, were delighted in helping to celebrate their marriage, and here they were standing in front of each and every one of them pretending to be in love…pretending that they had something to celebrate when all along the whole relationship had been just a sham.

Brad put an arm around Paige and pulled her into his side. 'On behalf of my wife and I,' he began, with a humorous, teasing glint in his voice, 'I'd just like to say thank you, firstly to Rosie and Mike for going to so much trouble to organise this, and then to all of you. It's wonderful to see you all and have you share in our celebration.'

He turned and looked at Paige.

A warm summer breeze stirred the long grass in the paddock beside them. The smell of wood smoke drifted across the lawn.

Brad's eyes moved over her face, as if storing away the details of her features—the generous, soft curve of her lips, the large blue eyes fringed with dark, thick lashes.

'It doesn't seem like a whole year since we got married, does it?' he reflected softly. 'But I'd just like to say that it has been one of the happiest years of my life… Thank you, Paige.'

Everyone clapped and cheered as he bent and kissed her softly on the lips.

Paige's eyes brimmed with tears. She was holding onto her emotions now by just a thread.

How could Brad look at her so tenderly when only this morning he had been planning to go away with somebody else? She still couldn't believe it of him. No matter what differences they had, she had always thought that he was sincere, that he tried his utmost for truth, for decency.

Mike handed William over to Brad for a moment.

'Just look after him while I go and see to the barbecue,' he said with a grin. 'Get some practice in.'

'Now, that would be my pleasure.' Brad smiled down at the baby. 'Hello, little man, how are you?'

The baby looked up at him, all cute dimples and sunny smiles.

'Not like the same child we took shopping, is he, Paige?' Rosie laughed. 'You'll make a good father, Brad.'

'I hope so,' Brad acknowledged gently. 'I'm certainly looking forward to it.' His eyes moved over towards Paige.

'Excuse me.' Paige could hold in her tears no longer. She hurried past the people and out towards the privacy of the apple trees at the bottom of the garden.

She took deep, shuddering breaths as tears started to flow freely down her cheeks.

'Paige…' Brad came after her, catching her as she rounded the corner and pulling her towards him. 'Paige…?'

He looked down at her and his eyes darkened. 'Oh, honey, don't cry. Please.'

'I can't help it.' She shook her head and tried very hard to stop, but her breathing caught on painful sobs.

'What can I do to make it better?' He reached and pulled her into his arms and for a while she rested against him gratefully. 'Come on, sweetheart,' he soothed her gently.

She couldn't get her breath to answer him, to say anything.

'Is the thought of spending the rest of your life with me really so abhorrent?' he asked, pulling back and looking down, deep into her eyes.

'Under…under these circumstances…' She nodded and tried to find a tissue in her bag.

'Here.' He handed her a handkerchief. 'Paige, don't

ask me to let you go.' His voice was so sad, so anguished that it tore at her completely.

'I...I know you want your child, Brad. I know how much it means to you, but we can't live a lie.' She brushed the handkerchief over her eyes and tried desperately to pull herself together.

She looked up at him gently. 'I know deep down that you've got the best of intentions at heart, wanting to look after me...wanting to stay with me because of our baby. I know you're a good man, Brad—'

'But you don't love me.' He looked at her bleakly. 'I know I bullied you into marrying me...that it was never really what you wanted. Don't think I haven't chastised myself for it many, many times over this last year. I shouldn't have rushed you...forced you into something when you weren't thinking straight...when you had very few choices open to you. And I'm sorry that the baby has made you feel tied to me.' He groaned and shook his head. 'But I just wanted you so damn much.'

Paige stared up at him. 'You didn't want me at all... You wanted Carolyn.'

For a second Brad just looked at her blankly. 'Paige, that's just not true.'

'Don't do this, Brad.' Paige took a step back from him. 'I know you want to make things right for me, that you want your child, but don't try to cover up the truth. I don't want you to protect me from it. How could any of us be happy when you are in love with someone else?'

'Paige.' He took hold of her arms and stared down at her. 'I love you...I've always loved you.'

She shook her head, not daring to believe him. 'Our marriage was a business arrangement,' she reminded him, her voice broken with distress. 'Meant to be for one year only. You married me on the rebound from Carolyn when you felt you had nothing else to lose.'

'Let me tell you something, Paige. I never loved

Carolyn… I dated her, sure, but I made it clear that I was never going to get involved because deep down I knew it was always you. I just didn't want to make a move on you until you'd finished college. But then Carolyn started to get serious and I didn't want to hurt her any more than I already had, so I told her we couldn't see each other any more. That was the month before you were due home… Then all your father's problems came to a head and instead of being able to date you…suddenly I was the enemy.'

'You finished with Carolyn?' She could hardly take in what he was telling her.

'Well don't sound so surprised,' he drawled with a grin. 'All right, I didn't go around shouting about the fact; it would hardly have been gallant, would it? But besides that I did feel a bit guilty where she was concerned. I never lied to her, but she was pretty cut up when I ended it—rushed off and married Robert Hicks.'

'But I saw her in your arms that night of our benefit party… I thought you were still in love with her.'

'Oh, Paige!' His eyes moved tenderly over her. 'She was in a bad state…crying and so unhappy…and she turned to me for advice. That was why she came to see me a couple of times at the office as well. We used to be friends and I thought I owed her the courtesy of listening to her, but there was nothing romantic about it… Hell, quite the opposite. I felt so damn sorry for her.'

'You really don't love her?' Paige whispered. 'I thought when she came to the house yesterday that you were really upset.'

He frowned. 'She came over to tell me about some settlement Robert had offered her. Some property and an income. Wanted to get my advice. The only thing that upset me yesterday afternoon was the way you had to force yourself to say that we were both pleased about the baby. I thought you were feeling trapped and un-happy.'

Paige stared at him. 'And I thought that Carolyn's visit was part of some big charade, that you were pretending to finish with her while secretly planning an affair. In fact every time you've been late home or had to go into town unexpectedly I've thought you were seeing her.'

'Paige, get it into your head.' He lifted her chin and looked into her eyes. 'I finished with Carolyn a long, long time ago. There is absolutely nothing between us any more. I love you.'

Paige didn't know whether to cry or laugh or what to say. 'But what about our one-year contract? When you proposed you acted as if you really didn't care whether I accepted you or not. You even said that if the engagement ring didn't fit we could forget the whole thing.'

He smiled now and his eyes moved tenderly over the sweetness of her features. 'Paige, darling, if that ring hadn't fitted you I would have had the size altered pretty damn quick and asked you again. I was trying to hide behind a façade of indifference because I believed that if you knew exactly how much I wanted you, you'd laugh in my face and run in the opposite direction, straight into your college friend's arms just to spite me. You were so angry with me, Paige, and I didn't know what to do to try and keep you. So I set out to entice you, catch you before you could escape. I hoped that when the pain of your father's death started to ease you might turn to me willingly, might fall in love with me, and that we could forget our one-year-only arrangement and make it for ever.' He looked down at her lovingly. 'Please believe me, sweetheart... I've always loved you. Carolyn was only ever a friend as far as I was concerned.'

He bent his head and kissed her gently. She clung to

him, drinking in the warmth of his love, so happy that she could hardly believe it.

He released her and looked down into her eyes. 'I know you feel trapped and that if it wasn't for the baby you would be walking away from me right now. But I want you so damn much. I want our baby, our marriage. They are the most important things in the world to me... You are the most important thing in the world.'

She reached up and touched a gentle finger to his lips. 'You don't know how much I've dreamed of hearing you say those words,' she said huskily. 'I love you so much, Brad. I always have, but I believed you loved someone else.'

She could see the joy in his eyes as she said those words, heard the catch in his breath as he pulled her close into his arms.

'I thought I'd rushed you into something you didn't want and I tried so damn hard to be patient and not scare you off,' he murmured huskily against her ear. 'But Lord, sometimes I was just so damn scared that you never would turn to me and that you still wanted Josh.'

'I've never wanted Josh, Brad. There was never anything between us. He was a friend, nothing more. I should have said something before but my pride wouldn't let me. I guess I just wanted you to be jealous.'

Brad looked surprised then held her tight.

For a long while there was silence as they kissed, the feeling, the love that flowed between them taking Paige's body by storm so that she could only lean weakly against him. She wondered if she was dreaming, if any moment she would wake up and this wouldn't really be happening. It was just so amazing, so wonderful.

'Hey, you two lovebirds.' Rosie's voice interrupted them as she came around the corner. She came to a standstill and then grinned as she saw them. 'Do you want to eat this afternoon or are you already on your first course?'

Paige stepped back from Brad, her cheeks glowing, her eyes wide with happiness. 'We're coming,' she said unsteadily.

'I should think so,' Rosie replied. 'You lucky things will have ten whole days to canoodle to your hearts' content once you get to the Bahamas—'

'Hey, big mouth!' Brad complained with a laugh. 'That was supposed to be a surprise!'

'Oh! Sorry.' Rosie pulled a wry face and clapped a hand to her mouth. 'Never was much good at secrets, was I, Paige...?' She grinned at her friend. 'So what do you think...fabulous present or what? I was green with envy when Brad told me on the phone this morning.'

'You were talking to Rosie on the phone this morning?' Paige looked up at Brad.

'Yeah, well, Rosie did let it slip to me about her plans for today so we thought we may as well liaise about the details.'

'I can't believe that I've been such a fool,' Paige murmured as she thought about her terrible suspicions. She went into her husband's arms with a heartfelt sigh. 'Oh, Brad, I love you so, so much.'

'OK...I get the hint...' Rosie laughed and turned back towards the house. 'Dig into the food, folks,' Paige heard her calling out laughingly. 'Our guests of honour might be some considerable time.'

'Maybe we'd better go back and join the party,' Paige said after a while, her lips swollen from Brad's kisses, her heart swollen with love.

'Maybe we should,' Brad said gently.

'Before we do I want to give you my present.' Paige opened up her handbag and took out the small, gift-wrapped package.

She watched as he opened it.

'It's not as exciting as a trip to the Bahamas,' she said shyly. 'But I thought you'd like it.'

'It's wonderful,' he said sincerely as he looked at the gold wristwatch. Then he looked into her eyes. 'And very significant, now that we've got all the time in the world to be together...' He reached to kiss her again. 'Happy anniversary, darling.'

# Take 2 bestselling love stories FREE

## Plus get a FREE surprise gift!

---

## Special Limited-Time Offer

**Mail to Harlequin Reader Service®**

> 3010 Walden Avenue
> P.O. Box 1867
> Buffalo, N.Y. 14240-1867

**YES!** Please send me 2 free Harlequin Presents® novels and my free surprise gift. Then send me 6 brand-new novels every month, which I will receive months before they appear in bookstores. Bill me at the low price of $3.12 each plus 25¢ delivery and applicable sales tax, if any*. That's the complete price, and a saving of over 10% off the cover prices—quite a bargain! I understand that accepting the books and gift places me under no obligation ever to buy any books. I can always return a shipment and cancel at any time. Even if I never buy another book from Harlequin, the 2 free books and the surprise gift are mine to keep forever.

106 HEN CH69

---

Name _____ (PLEASE PRINT)

Address _____ Apt. No. _____

City _____ State _____ Zip _____

This offer is limited to one order per household and not valid to present Harlequin Presents® subscribers. *Terms and prices are subject to change without notice. Sales tax applicable in N.Y.

*The only way to be a bodyguard is to stay as close as a lover...*

# STAND BY ME

The relationship between bodyguard and client is always close...sometimes too close for comfort. This September, join in the adventure as three bodyguards, protecting three very distracting and desirable charges, struggle not to cross the line between business and pleasure.

## STRONG ARMS OF THE LAW
### by Dallas SCHULZE

## NOT WITHOUT LOVE
### by Roberta LEIGH

## SOMETIMES A LADY
### by Linda Randall WISDOM

*Sometimes danger makes a strange bedfellow!*

Available September 1998 wherever Harlequin and Silhouette books are sold.

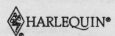 

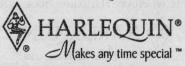

# Toast the special events in your life with Harlequin Presents®!

With the purchase of *two* Harlequin Presents® BIG EVENT books, you can send in for two sparkling plum-colored Wineglasses. A retail value of $19.95!

## ACT NOW TO COLLECT
## TWO BEAUTIFUL WINEGLASSES!

On the official proof-of-purchase coupon below, fill in your name, address and zip or postal code and send it, plus $2.99 U.S./$3.99 CAN. for postage and handling (check or money order—please do not send cash) payable to Harlequin Books, to: In the U.S.: 3010 Walden Avenue, P.O. Box 9077, Buffalo, N.Y. 14269-9077; In Canada: P.O. Box 609, Fort Erie, Ontario L2A 5X3. Please allow 4-6 weeks for delivery. Order your set of wineglasses now! Quantities are limited. Offer for the Plum Wineglasses expires December 31, 1998.

---

## Harlequin Presents®—The Big Event!

### OFFICIAL PROOF OF PURCHASE

**"Please send me my TWO Wineglasses"**

Name: _____

Address: _____

City: _____

State/Prov.: _____ Zip/Postal Code: _____

Account Number: _____ 097 KGS CSA6 193-3

---

HPBEPOP

# HARLEQUIN®
*Makes any time special* ™

 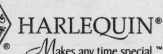